One Enchanted Scottish Knight

by

Laura Strickland

This is a work of fiction. Names, characters, places, and incidents are either the product of the author's imagination or are used fictitiously, and any resemblance to actual persons living or dead, business establishments, events, or locales, is entirely coincidental.

One Enchanted Scottish Knight

COPYRIGHT © 2019 by Laura Strickland

The Wild Rose Press, Inc.
PO Box 708
Adams Basin, NY 14410-0708
Visit us at www.thewildrosepress.com

Publishing History
First Tea Rose Edition, 2019
Print ISBN 978-1-5092-2663-4
Digital ISBN 978-1-5092-2664-1

Published in the United States of America

This man wore darkness. She saw it in his hair—a fall of straight black locks loose upon his shoulders—and in the eyes that met hers briefly before he focused on her bloody hand.

She'd sensed that darkness in him when he rode down on the crossroads, a thing of spirit as much as appearance. Some great trouble or sorrow rode within him. For all that, she sensed no cruelty. And och, aye, he carried beauty also.

Had she ever seen such a countenance? Narrow and elegantly sculpted as that of a raptor, his face tapered from sharp cheekbones to a strong jaw now well covered by black beard.

Above those eyes—black as the gaze of a raven—slanted two eyebrows like wings, fleet and mobile. Even as she watched they drew together over his bulwark of a nose, and black lashes swept down.

"Forgive me. I must have cut you when I slashed those ties. Let me see—how sore is it?"

He smoothed away the blood with strong, graceful fingers—touched her blood, her being—and Tansy quivered again. For an instant she felt so dizzy she feared she might tumble from the great horse's back, but the knight's arm anchored her.

She found her voice. "A small price to pay, Sir Knight. Would you no' say?"

That returned his eyes to hers. They gazed at one another so intimately, so deeply, Tansy felt a connection take hold between them.

Was that just the last remnant of the spell she'd woven, vibrating? She could not tell.

Praise for Laura Strickland

Laura Strickland's novella *FORGED BY LOVE* won first place in the short historical category of the International Digital Awards.

~*~

"The world building is phenomenal."
~Daysie W. at My Book Addiction and More

~*~

"Laura Strickland creates a world that not only draws you in, but she incorporates it…seamlessly. …the kind of book that keeps you awake well into the wee hours, and sighing with satisfaction when you've finished the very last page."

~Nicole McCaffrey, author

~*~

"As I read I became so involved with the story, I found it difficult to put down the book. …Definitely …an author to watch."

~Dandelion at Long & Short Reviews

~*~

"Laura Strickland takes us beyond the fairy tale and ballroom and gives the readers a story full of pain and heartbreak, wonderfully balanced with hope and love."

~Elissa Blabac, InD'tale Magazine

~*~

"What follows will make you cry, angry, and appreciative of your own life."

~Lisa O'Connor, Author and Reviewer

Chapter One

Aberdeenshire, Scotland, June 1597

Tansy Bellrose Gant gasped and struggled as the thin leather twine closed around the tender skin at her wrists. Her captors pulled the bond cruelly tight and dragged her roughly toward the post that stood at the middle of the crossroads. A wave of helplessness swamped her. Tansy did not appreciate feeling helpless, and her emotions further escalated on a wave of disbelief. Those who wrestled her into submission were not strangers but her neighbors, the good men of Slurt—the town where she'd been born and raised.

It occurred to her, like a sun bursting in her brain, she may have overstepped herself this time. Quite possibly she'd gone just a wee bit too far in her bid to shame that hag Ranna Farquharson, and so abandoned the bounds of caution…or wisdom. The demon that all too often took up residence in her heart—not the Devil himself, surely, but rather the imp known as mischief—had got the better of her again.

Did it not always?

Ever since she'd been a small lass, as far back as she could remember, she'd had a tendency to get herself into trouble on a regular basis. She'd been making up wild stories since almost before she could speak, talking about companions no one else could see, playing tricks on folk for the sheer pleasure of watching them sweat and squirm.

And wanting things she could not—or should not—have. That, most of all.

Her stepmother, Bessie, who'd raised her after her own mother ran away, despaired of her right early. Not that Bessie had ever been anything but kind. A bright image of her homely face flashed into Tansy's mind even as her neighbors slammed her up against the post and true fear touched her for the first time.

What would Bessie say when she found out Tansy had been handed over by the people of Slurt to the Royal Commission, for trial as a witch? For that was what these neighbors threatened to do. Poor Bessie would likely weep and despair all over again. For even here in Slurt they'd heard of the fervor for persecution that seized most of Scotland in this, the year of 1597. Folk sent away to the Commission for questioning and trial seldom returned. And there had been lurid accounts of just what went on during questioning—enough to force Tansy's stomach to turn in a slow roll.

Defying the fear, she bared her teeth and threw back her head, testing the strength of her bonds and the men who held her.

"I am no witch! Willie MacTay, you have known me all your life."

"Aye." Willie rolled his eyes like a terrified pony. "And I ken fine you get up to some damn strange things, Tansy Bellrose. Milk curdles when you walk past. Roosters fall silent. Those you look on with those queerly colored eyes o' yours take ill."

"Careful she does no' hex you now," cautioned his companion and cohort, Rafe Leslie. Those two, along with Rafe's brother, Ronnie, had wrangled Tansy out of the village market—where, admittedly, she'd gone to make some trouble for that shrew Ranna—and here to the crossroads and the stone post to which she now stood affixed.

This was all Ranna's fault. Or nay—'twas the fault of that young buck Ossian Bain, for being so handsome. Tansy should have just let Ranna have him.

"Queerly colored eyes?" she repeated on a wave of combined alarm and offended pride. "Ye did no' fear them last year, Rafe Leslie, when you asked me to walk out wi' you."

Could that be what all this was about? Most of the young men of Slurt—admittedly not plentiful in number—had asked Tansy to step out with them at one time or another. She'd soundly spurned them all.

"Do not let her look at you, laddie," cautioned Willie again, in a hoarse growl. "She'll magic you sure and make you let her go."

Fine chance of it, thought Tansy, her heart beating so hard she found it difficult to breathe. For down the road from the village came half the population of the clachan, neighbors and—aye—some members of Tansy's family, abandoning the market to come see what transpired. Slurt being so small, it might empty all its contents and yet not fill the place where these two roads met.

Tansy prickled all over with the humiliation of it. She did not want everyone to see her thus—tied up like a sow, caught fine and in the hands of Willie, who hadn't washed himself in three years and was not likely to soon.

Here came her father, a tall man, his hair—as she

suddenly saw—gone gray, looking as worried as Tansy had ever seen him. Along behind, puffing with the effort to keep up, came Bessie, her brown hair escaping its cap, her face contorted by distress. Bessie must have abandoned her stall, and she only did that under the most extreme circumstances.

Tansy's guts clenched hard. Extreme, indeed.

Ah, and here came Ranna Farquharson, striving to look demure and as if butter wouldn't melt in her mouth, but with a flush of victory in her cheeks and a gleam in her blue eyes.

So Ranna thought to get rid of Tansy thus, did she? And have Ossian for her own.

Tansy fixed her eyes on Ranna and narrowed them. It might have been unwise for her to provoke Ranna this morning. But how was she to know something as ugly as a witch hunt could ensue here in this peaceful fold of the Scottish countryside?

Tansy intensified her stare, and Ranna tripped over a nonexistent stone. Despite her alarm, Tansy flushed with satisfaction.

"What goes on here?" called Tansy's father, even before he reached them. "Willie MacTay, take your hands from my daughter."

"I will not," Willie called back, and Tansy heard the fear in his voice. Fear of her, Tansy, or her father? Could well be either, Drachan Gant being a powerfully built man who'd worked hard on his croft all his life.

But Willie turned to face him, the other young men who'd captured Tansy moving up to stand with him shoulder to shoulder.

Drachan, his face as white as Bessie's was red, marched up to them and immediately tried to reach for

Tansy. A struggle ensued, mostly pushing and shoving, with a few blows cast, during which Tansy found herself pushed hard against the stone post. For an instant she could not get her breath, and her head reeled till the pressure eased. The young men of the village had closed ranks around her.

"Do no' let him get to her!" Ronnie Leslie cried.

"Hold!"

The cry contained authority and froze everyone where he or she stood. Stephen Farquharson, being the mill owner, fancied himself headman of the clachan, and no one had ever disputed that claim. Father to the lovely Ranna, he answered only to the local laird.

Tansy frowned. If they hauled her off to face the laird—a sanctimonious old stoat—she could not expect to fare well. Of course, 'twould be better than being turned over to the Royal Commission or to the King himself, who seemed to have a real bug up his bum when it came to the subject of witches.

Now Stephen—wide of girth as befitted his wealth—caught up with his daughter, Ranna, who after one victorious look at Tansy kept her eyes cast to the ground.

Tansy's father whirled and faced off against the miller. "What is this, Stephen?" Drachan cried. "Tell them to let my daughter go."

"I cannot." Stephen Farquharson spoke sorrowfully and shook his head. "She has been accused of witchcraft."

A small cry escaped Bessie who, like Farquharson, had caught up. She now stepped to Tansy's side and laid a hand on her shoulder.

A brave act, as Tansy knew. Those who openly

associated with accused witches often stood trial alongside them.

"No," Bessie said—only that, but it made her husband look at her and caused Tansy to catch back a groan.

Ah, and she had been a sore trial to them all this while—the wild daughter of a runaway hoyden, at such variance with their own children who came later. She might just as well have been a magpie in Bessie's nest.

Tears filled her eyes. Curse it all! She seldom wept for any reason and hated that she'd been pushed to it now. But fear seemed to have a terrible grip on her, and the scene blurred before her eyes.

As did her father's face when he stepped up toe to toe with Stephen Farquharson.

"You know us for a godly family, Stephen," Drachan asserted. "Braw members of the kirk. 'Tis madness, this accusation."

"'Tis madness, all of it!" Bessie declared. "What has been happening in Edinburgh and farther north—I canna' believe you would condone that here, Master Farquharson!"

Stephen bent a hard look on Bessie, and her fingers dug painfully into Tansy's shoulder.

"Mistress, this 'madness' as you call it has infested our nation for a reason. The King hi'sel' has taken up the cause of scourging evil frae the land. Can we here in Slurt do any less?"

"But Tansy…" Bessie protested.

Farquharson switched his gaze back to Tansy's father. "Drachan, I say nothing against your family. But you maun admit, strange things have aye happened with Tansy by. What of Nallan's goat?"

"What of it?" Drachan demanded. "'Twas just a goat."

"One that would nae stay at home for following your daughter around, high and low, day and night. And then it had a two-headed kid. There are other evils as well. You ken fine the mill wheel always wobbles when she walks by. Magpies gather on the roof of your house. If someone speaks amiss to her, their stock sickens. And only this day she did speak a curse to my daughter, Ranna, at the market." He gestured wildly to Ranna. "Here, lass, and tell."

Tansy's heart fell violently, though she hadn't thought it could sink lower. Aye, Ranna would tell right enough—she must be falling over herself to make the accusation.

Ranna stepped forward as bidden, the look of false innocence still pasted to her face. Eyes downcast, she took the place beside her father and spoke in a near whisper.

"I do not like to say, Father. I dare not repeat such words."

Nay, she would make them drag it from her and be all the more convincing.

At that moment, another individual came pushing through the crowd, which now truly did contain nearly all the residents of the clachan. Tall and robust, his fair head topped most of the others, and his broad shoulders cleared the way. Ossian Bain must have come straight from his father's stall at the market. Aye, here came the elder Master Bain hurrying behind him.

Tansy's heart beat double time beneath her breast. Would Ossian speak up for her? Would he declare himself at last?

To be sure, he'd been paying Tansy attention for years, since the both of them grew old enough to understand just what men and women got up to together. There had never been anyone for Tansy but the tall, blue-eyed lad with the handsome face and sunny nature. But Ranna had always been in the way, with her sly looks and her tempting dowry. Tansy and Ossian had shared far more than kisses, for Ossian— though a decent lad—had long since succumbed to Tansy's persuasions. She'd been certain her favors, combined with a few whispered charms, must make him offer marriage, in the end.

Now, held in the hard grip of neighbors-turned-enemies, she wondered if the moment had come, if this dangerous horror might make Ossian speak the words for which she'd waited so long. If he did speak up, declared for her, would that be enough to provide her protection?

She fixed her gaze on him and, with all her being, willed him to speak. Everyone else stared at him also. The noisy crowd grew so silent Tansy heard a magpie cry far off in the distance.

Speak, she ordered Ossian silently, calling up all the conviction inside her.

Ossian's lips parted in his flushed face. His gaze slid over Stephen Farquharson, Ranna, and the men holding Tansy before his blue eyes met with Tansy's to the exclusion of all else.

Despite her dire situation, Tansy's heart rose.

Give me my heart's desire…

"What goes on here?" Ossian asked. "Wha' has Tansy Bellrose done now?"

Chapter Two

"Hush, lad," Ossian's father, Doylan Bain, roared. Master Bain owned the finest team of horses in Slurt and went about helping his neighbors with their plowing, which made him a highly respected man. "Do no' involve yoursel' in this."

Ossian did not stir from the place he occupied, which happened to be right next to Ranna. The miller's daughter reached out and touched Ossian's arm. Only a fleeting gesture, yet the possessive expression that came to her face and the victorious look she darted at Tansy screamed aloud.

Ossian's father and Ranna's were fast friends. They'd long wished to join their families together through the marriage of their son and daughter. Ossian had declared—at least to Tansy—that he'd prefer otherwise, and Tansy had believed him.

Perhaps that had been another mistake.

Master Farquharson told the Bains, "My lass Ranna was about to tell us of the curse this witch bespoke in the market today."

Ossian flinched. His blue eyes widened, and the brilliant color ebbed from his cheek. He took a careful step backward.

Tansy knew the truth then, as if the tiny voice that sometimes whispered—and sometimes shouted—in the back of her mind declared it outright. Ossian Bain might be bonny. He might be long and strong of limb, and his kisses might taste like honey, but he had not the courage God gave a kirk mouse.

Despair, anger, and extreme disappointment all arose, tangled together in her breast. They might as well leave her tied to this post and set her alight now—her dearest desire being lost to her.

But she wanted to live, she wanted to live.

She fixed an unblinking stare on Ranna's face, daring the wretched lass to speak. They had hated each other since they were six and Ranna had taunted Tansy for having a mother who ran away rather than stay and raise her.

Nobody loves you, Ranna had declared, nasty even at that tender age. *Nobody ever will.*

But Bessie loved her, and Da, and her younger half-brothers and sisters, though they didn't understand her any more than a blind priest understood the sunrise.

Ossian—aye, maybe she'd been mistaken in him. And it looked to cost her dear now.

The Royal Commission. Questioning—the pain and humiliation of it so terrible it would make a body confess to things that weren't true, just to end the agony.

She struggled suddenly to draw a breath. Could that truly happen to her? Could it?

She increased the intensity of her glare at Ranna, who treated Tansy to one flash of burning hatred before lowering her lashes once more.

"Father, I do hate to say…I fear to repeat such words, for peril to my soul."

"Daughter, you must. Your kirk demands it, and your Crown. Justice demands it. If the heart of this woman be evil, the rest of us must be protected."

"My lass is no' evil." Drachan spoke up. "You lot ha' known her all her life."

"And her mother before her," Stephen Farquharson challenged. Rafe Leslie's grip on Tansy tightened painfully. "What was she, Drachan, who went awa' wi' the fairies?"

Da's face darkened. "The sins o' the mother are no' those of the child."

"Has she the mark o' the Devil?" asked Ronnie Leslie, close beside his brother. "Let us strip her naked and see."

"Nay!" Bessie cried, and Tansy's legs threatened to give way beneath her.

"Nay," Master Farquharson confirmed. "'Tis a task for the Commission, that. They will ferret out the truth."

"Aye, so," said Da, truly angry now, angrier than Tansy had ever seen him. He too fixed his gaze on Ranna. "Let us hear this accusation."

Silence fell again. Tansy heard only the wind sighing over the land and wished she could fly away with it. But she stood lashed securely to the post, with her captors hedging her in.

Ranna raised eyes naked with hate to Tansy's face. "She said to me this very day she hoped the hair would fall from my head, the teeth from my mouth, and I would wither and die like a sprig of heather in the killing frost!"

Gasps greeted those words—a damning cluster of them, and no mistake. The wishing of illness or death could not be taken lightly, and horror touched every visage, including Tansy's own.

Master Farquharson turned on her. "Did you speak these words, lass?"

"I did not." In truth, what she'd said had been far more poetic, as well as damning. Best Ranna could not recite accurately what Tansy had actually said so rashly. They would not wait for the Commission but would burn her to death here and now.

"She did." Rafe Leslie stepped up beside Ranna. "I was standing nearby and heard her."

Tansy switched her glare to him. "You were but hanging about because you wished to get up Ranna's skirt—you wish it still! That is why you speak now."

It might be an exaggeration, but Tansy fought for her life.

"Nay," Rafe began, but Ranna interrupted him. Hatred, raw and certain, now flooded her whole face.

"Everyone here knows what you are, Tansy Bellrose Gant. You wished me harm—deny that!"

Tansy could not, in good faith. She would lie though, if she must.

She spat at Ranna, "You are but saying these words because you want him." She jerked her chin at Ossian Bain. "And you ken fine he wants me instead."

Ranna stepped toward her. "I am saying it because you are an evil sickness in our midst that needs to be scourged. May you travel straight to the Devil where you belong!"

Murmurs broke out among the onlookers; a chant began. "Evil! Witch!"

Bessie spread her arms and tried to step between Tansy and danger. Da as swiftly pushed her aside and interposed his tall body; for an instant Tansy felt wondrously sheltered. But, with a grunt, Wille MacTay swung round and knocked Da down with the kind of punch that might fell a man twice his size.

Bessie screamed. Ronnie used his body to push Tansy hard against the post, and Master Farquharson bellowed, "Do not let them free her! Holding her for the Royal Commission is of utmost importance. Word shall be sent this very day."

"But what to do wi' her meanwhile, Master Farquharson?" asked Rafe, who still hovered at Ranna's side, even as Ossian stood at her other shoulder. Master Farquharson pondered the question, while Bessie dropped to her knees at Da's side.

At last Farquharson cried, "Leave her tied to the post. Make certain she cannot wiggle free, even through the use of magic. Be sure not to look her in the eyes, lest she cast a spell! She will harm you if she can."

"Nay!" wailed Bessie. But she remained on the ground while the Leslie brothers checked the bonds that tied Tansy to the post, drawing them still tighter, so they bit cruelly into her flesh.

Despite the pain, she struggled. She wanted very badly to reach her Da, who lay senseless, with blood trickling down his face, so she kicked out, using her feet to best advantage, landing blows where she could. She wailed like a dark spirit and her black hair, never well disciplined, tumbled down her back like that of a wild woman.

The crowd, as if irresistibly drawn, moved closer, Ranna and her father still at the forefront. Tansy wished right enough she could fell Ranna there and then, as Willie had Da—scratch her blooming cheeks, cause her to wither with every kind of pain. But fear had her by the throat so hard she could only wail, and terror threatened to steal the very sense from her mind.

Roughly, the Leslie brothers ran their hands over her before stepping back to view their handiwork. The marker, a pillar of stone ragged enough to tear the skin from Tansy's back, stood six or seven feet tall. The lettering on one side, as Tansy well knew, read Slurt. That on the east face read Stirling. Tansy, pinned against it, had nowhere to hide.

She searched the faces of her neighbors—folk she'd known all her life—for a shred of mercy and found none. Instead, these folk gazed at her as upon a stranger, with rampant hatred, suspicion, and incipient enjoyment.

She laid her head back against the post and flung her gaze to the far horizon.

Escape. Escape!

A magpie, black marked with blue and white, flew across the skyline. Tansy's heart bounded perilously. *One brings sorrow, and one brings joy...* Despite the bird's prophecy of grief, she wished she might fly with it, stream away, find her strength and power...disappear into freedom.

Take me, she whispered to the knowing that dwelt inside her. *Lift me.*

Save me.

Chapter Three

The road looked like all the others Malcolm Montgomery had traveled since leaving Dun Ballan, where he'd lately been imprisoned—narrow, hedged by flowering bushes, and backed by rolling fields and hills. He could not say what set all his senses on alert or caused him to check his weary horse and search the stretch just ahead.

Two rows of puddles remained after last night's rain, and a rise kept him from seeing very far.

His mount—one of Latham's animals given to him for his task—snorted and blew. Once fresh, the animal no doubt now felt as spent as Malcom did, for he ached with bone-deep weariness kept at bay only by iron determination.

This road, to the best of his estimation, led straight northward, though certainly he had never ridden it before. Northward—homeward—had been his chosen direction ever since his release from Latham's dungeon.

Upon that thought, and in defiance of the pleasant day, he began to sweat as he did each time he remembered the black hole that had housed him...how many days? Faith and he'd lost count.

He dragged in a deep lungful of clean air and let his eyes follow the flight of a bird on the horizon. He'd been unable to breathe properly in the dungeon. A few days longer and he might well have lost his senses.

And his brother, Mercien—most beloved person in Malcolm's world—languished in Dun Ballan still, in a hole no doubt identical to the one Malcolm had occupied.

That bastard, Latham, had not permitted Malcolm to see Mercien—nay, that would have been too merciful, too heartening. Latham would not understand the advantage of a kind gesture if it walked up and slapped him.

Nay, he'd but given Malcolm the chance to ransom his brother in the most impossible of ways.

And now Malcolm could feel something ahead, just over the rise in the road, that both called to him and made him want to turn his horse around and ride as fast as he could in the opposite direction.

Trouble.

He'd always had an instinct for it. It had served him and Mercien well in battle when they fought together under Lord Turney's banner. Before Lord Turney had fallen, that was, and his lands were confiscated by the King. Before Mercien got himself captured for love of a woman, and the world, as both Montgomery brothers knew it, fell apart.

Women. God defend him from them!

He drew another breath and concentrated on the sensation that slithered down the road toward him. A calling. An invitation. A demand.

He recognized the longing contained in that call—the same that had possessed him when, chained to the dungeon wall, he'd ached to be set free. It spoke to him so loudly he urged his horse forward with his knees, leaving his hands free to slide his sword from its scabbard.

This sword had traveled with him to France and back, fighting other men's battles, and when Latham had returned it to him, he'd sworn it would be raised hereafter only in his own or his family's service. But his heart trembled at the force of what came to him down that narrow lane. And instinct far stronger than intention took him forward.

The scene burst upon his eyes as soon as he crested the hill. A throng of people occupied a crossroads just ahead. He could see a tiny clachan beyond, its peacefulness so at variance with the rest of the scene he could scarcely reconcile it. The noise found him likewise—screaming and hollering, voices raised in what sounded like anger and protest. The emotions, too, rushed at him, all too close to what he'd felt in his confinement.

Anger. Despair.

He slowed his horse once more, seeking for wisdom. He should ride on, skirt this dire situation with all its trouble, for God knew he had trouble enough of his own. One thing stopped him.

A figure stood lashed to the pillar at the center of the crossroads.

Even at this distance, he knew it for a woman, a slender figure with wild black hair tumbled over her shoulders, tied to the post. The desperation and agony he sensed stemmed directly from her, feelings so powerful they slammed into him like a crashing wave. The other figures danced around her like devils round a bonfire. Even at a distance of thirty paces Malcolm registered their eagerness, their glee.

What unholy thing took place here in this bucolic place?

Naught to him.

He told himself so even as he once more urged his mount forward, drawn by curiosity and that odd sense of compulsion. Everything seemed to slow down. He could hear the voices of the folk gathered around the post—like the cries of birds—sharp with excitement and something else far less savory. He saw what looked like glee as their faces turned toward him; he felt the impact—like a hard blow to the gut—as the woman tied to the post looked up and her gaze met his.

Aye, and it might as well be a blow; the desperation he'd sensed all the way down the road roared from her, bright as pain or the light reflected from a battle shield. Her eyes, silver as any shield, looked uncanny, terrified—fey.

"What goes on here?" he called out, and the crowd went silent, like a field of barley when the wind dies. The sweating faces, most flushed, registered shock at his appearance. No one replied.

"I say, what is this madness?"

"Sir Knight!" A man stepped forward. Tall and rawboned, he had blood on his face and a wild look in his eye. "I beg for your succor. They have seized my daughter. They accuse her of witchcraft."

Witchcraft. For an instant the edges of Malcolm's world darkened; he flailed inwardly. The pursuit of witches had become a sickness in the land he loved and a blackness at its heart.

He hauled involuntarily at his mount's reins, and the animal danced a few steps. He looked at the woman tied to the post.

Young. So many of those accused were aged grannies guilty of nothing more than imagined slights—

not a bit of evil in them. He knew that too well. But to accuse this lass, her body bound against the post like a graceful willow bough, eyes great with longing, struck him hard. An abomination. But not his trouble, not at all.

The man reached for the bridle of Malcolm's horse. "Please, Sir Knight. They will send her to the Royal Commission for questioning."

Would they? To Malcolm, it looked more like they meant to burn her on the spot.

He called out, "Who is in charge here?"

Another man stepped forward. This one, stout and balding, wore good boots and a fine jacket. His face shone red with effort or annoyance.

"I am Stephen Farquharson, miller. This, Sir Knight, is a town matter and naught to do with you."

So it was. Malcolm experienced an almost overwhelming desire to ride away—leave these madmen and women to their unsavory pursuits.

But the lanky man still gripped his bridle and bent his gaze on Malcolm, beseeching.

"Please, Sir Knight, stop them."

"I have no power to stop them, my good man." Who was he to brandish authority? Just a dispossessed knight on an impossible quest.

"But my daughter, she is a good lass. A bit wayward at times, mayhap, like her mother..."

"Her mother," seethed a young woman, who might have been bonny if not for her sharp expression, "a witch of the first water, that one."

"Let the Commission decide," declared the stout man. "For, Sir Knight, this one did curse my daughter, and we dare no longer suffer her here in Slurt."

"Then turn her out along the open roads. The Commission is no' called for." Malcolm paused. From what he'd heard, he'd not wish to see a true witch fall into their hands. And the woman lashed to the post looked like naught more than an ordinary lass, even though Malcolm could feel the emotions streaming off her like steam from a kettle.

The stout man looked horrified. "Let her go? And have her come creeping back in the dead of night?"

Impatience touched Malcolm. He tried to free his reins from the lanky man's grasp and move around the post. "Leave go of me."

Please.

The word came in an agonized whisper, so soft that for a moment he doubted he'd heard anything at all. His head swiveled involuntarily, and his gaze found that of the accused witch.

By all that was holy! She truly had the most uncanny eyes he'd ever seen—silver, as he'd marked even from a distance, flashing bright. And they held an intensity that seemed to reach right inside him, take hold of his spirit, and bend it to her will.

A magpie called close overhead. Even the harsh sound failed to sunder the fierce connection that had fused itself to Malcolm's soul.

Please. Free me. Free—

Aye.

He brandished his already bared sword and jerked his horse's head free all in one movement. Two big, young louts stood guard at either side of the post. A strike to the arm eliminated one; the second shied away when Malcolm looked at him. He pressed his mount in close to the post, close enough to see naked hope flood the young woman's eyes. Close enough to slash the bonds that held her.

Everyone began shouting at once. The crowd rushed at Malcolm, and he turned the horse to ward them off. The woman leaped; he saw her fingers, slender and white, clutch at his stirrup. He hauled her up by the back of her dress and spun the horse to face the others, sword at the ready.

"Tansy, lass!" the lanky man cried.

The lass made no reply. Huddled in front of Malcolm on his saddle, she'd frozen like a rabbit before the fox. He could smell her terror. So could his mount. Weary as the animal might be, it danced again, forcing the mob back a few steps.

"This is the work of the Devil!" the stout man cried.

No doubt it was.

"She has enchanted you, Sir Knight. You will live to regret—"

Malcolm stayed to hear no more. He urged his mount away from the post, away from the crossroads and the howling crowd, back the way he'd come.

As for regret—a near-constant companion of his—he heeded it not.

Chapter Four

Tansy released the last threads of the spell she'd woven and struggled to haul breath into her lungs. Away—she'd gotten away from that horror, and her body still trembled in reaction. But whatever happened, she didn't want the knight with whom she now rode to guess she'd compelled him to release her, with magic.

The knight—oh, he'd appeared over the rise in the road like the answer to prayer, and deep abiding prayer at that. As soon as Tansy saw him she knew him for her way out.

He might even be more than that. From the tiny shards of excitement pricking her within, he might come to mean something significant. A way for her to leave Slurt, with its boredom and hatred.

And Ossian Bain?

A small ache of longing blossomed in her heart. There'd been a time when she felt sure she never wanted to leave the bonny Ossian. But he'd stood there like a great lump while their neighbors accused her. He would have seen her turned over to the Royal Commission for questioning.

A shudder quivered through her body, and her rescuer shifted a large hand—lodged protectively at her stomach—in response. He slowed his mount and looked down at her from a distance small enough to seem intimate.

"Are you all right, lass?"

For once in her life, Tansy didn't feel too certain. Profoundly shaken, she still found it difficult to breathe, and her wrist…

She brought it up from where it nestled in her skirt, only to see a bright smear of red. Blood. It invariably made Tansy dizzy—not because she was a delicate miss but because it sang a bold song she found hard to chase from her head.

She said, "I think…"

The knight swore. His hand—twice the size of hers and none too clean—came up and gently captured her wrist. His forbidding face frowned.

Forbidding face. So it was—one of the strongest and most intimidating Tansy had ever seen. Also one of the most handsome, in its way—not like Ossian, no, nothing like. Ossian seemed all brightness with his fair curls, blue eyes, and ruddy cheeks.

This man wore darkness. She saw it in his hair—a fall of straight black locks loose upon his shoulders—and in the eyes that met hers briefly before he focused on her bloody hand.

She'd sensed that darkness in him when he rode down on the crossroads, a thing of spirit as much as appearance. Some great trouble or sorrow rode within him. For all that, she sensed no cruelty. And och, aye, he carried beauty also.

Had she ever seen such a countenance? Narrow and elegantly sculpted as that of a raptor, his face tapered from sharp cheekbones to a strong jaw now well covered by black beard.

Above those eyes—black as the gaze of a raven—slanted two eyebrows like wings, fleet and mobile.

Even as she watched they drew together over his bulwark of a nose, and black lashes swept down.

"Forgive me. I must have cut you when I slashed those ties. Let me see—how sore is it?"

He smoothed away the blood with strong, graceful fingers—touched her blood, her being—and Tansy quivered again. For an instant she felt so dizzy she feared she might tumble from the great horse's back, but the knight's arm anchored her.

She found her voice. "A small price to pay, Sir Knight. Would you no' say?"

That returned his eyes to hers. They gazed at one another so intimately, so deeply, Tansy felt a connection take hold between them.

Was that just the last remnant of the spell she'd woven, vibrating? She could not tell.

His expression turned grim. "I would. Let us ride on to that wood up ahead, and we will pause to tend your wrist. I think there is some bandaging in my pack."

"Aye."

He urged the horse on, gently using his knees, clearly not thinking about the action. Ah, well, such men spent half their lives in the saddle, a life far beyond her ken.

She wondered who he served, where he might be bound, what miracle had brought him down that road when she needed him.

And just what he might mean to her life.

****

Malcolm could smell the lass who rode on the saddle in front of him, as good as in his arms. Indeed, she smelled of herbs, the remnants of her fear, and woman. Him, he'd become accustomed to the reek of fear in his opponents, in his comrades—in himself most recently.

He almost dismissed it now in favor of something else about this woman, something that screamed aloud, but that he didn't yet understand.

He seemed all too aware of her—each time she drew a breath or fluttered an eyelash, he noticed. And when she looked at him with her uncanny eyes, he felt it right down to his bones.

Fey, those eyes—clear and almost colorless, like water, they flashed silver and made a stark contrast with the lashes between which they were set, black as ink. He could almost believe her a witch as accused, given those eyes.

But, he reminded himself, eye color—like hair color, height, or indeed beauty—was an accident of birth which men tended to equate with the spirit within.

A fatal mistake.

He drew his horse up under the cover of the trees and dismounted. Before he could turn back to the lass, she slid down from his horse's back. Her legs gave way beneath her.

Terror, and its aftereffects, could do that to a body, as he might have told her. He helped her up gently, and they gazed at one another once more.

A tiny thing, she barely topped his shoulder and could not weigh eight stone. Yet she had a force about her, for all that. The black hair hugged her shoulders like a ragged shawl; her feet were bare.

She held her injured wrist tight to her breast; already the wound had begun to clot, blood ceasing to flow.

He spewed a relieved breath; at least he had not harmed her too sorely.

He turned to the pack lashed to his saddle and yanked it open, giving her a look from the corner of his eyes.

"What was that all about, back there?"

She seemed to ponder her answer carefully before she said, "Jealousy."

"Eh?" That lifted his brows.

"Two women," she said with surprising acerbity, "after the love of one man. Need you ask me more, Sir Knight?"

"It seems I must. What has that to do with an accusation of witchcraft?"

"My rival wanted rid of me, the vicious *chattan*."

"Ah. The question is how did this rival o' yours persuade the rest of the clachan to go along wi' it? That was your whole village, eh?" He jerked his head back toward Slurt.

"So it was." She pondered that also, and a new emotion appeared in her eyes. Hesitance? Grief? "Such things spread like sickness."

Aye, and there was a truth.

He drew a cloth from his pack and turned back to her. "Let me see that wound."

She lifted her hand trustingly. Her wrist, slender as that of a child, bore a deep gouge where the point of his sword had caught the flesh. Christ, he might well have slain her in his bold attempt at rescue. But he'd felt such a compulsion to save her and get her away from that place, he'd acted without thought.

"I am that sorry," he told her. "In my haste I slashed more than your bonds."

She tossed her head. "No' your fault. They were very tight, and needs must. I heal quickly and shall soon be made right. Bruises, scrapes, wounds of all sorts melt from me."

"A singularly fortunate gift." And one that might have served her ill in the hands of the Royal Commission during questioning. Quick-healing marks would surely prompt the infliction of more, and would arouse the worst suspicions.

Using water from his flask, he gently sponged away the blood and wrapped the cut tightly. She stood still throughout, stoical as any warrior receiving rough care on the field of battle.

"There. Let your miraculous healing take hold." He withdrew his fingers from her flesh and put away the bandaging carefully. "Have you a name?"

"Indeed, does not everyone?" She drew a breath. "I am Tansy Bellrose Gant."

That made his brows twitch. "An unusual appellation."

"Perhaps, but 'tis the only one I have."

That made him smile, almost against his will. Could he recall the last time he'd smiled? Aye, too well...

"And you, Sir Knight? Will you likewise share your name?"

"I am Malcolm Montgomery."

She inclined her head like a princess receiving a courtier. "Sir Malcolm."

"Is there somewhere I can escort you, Mistress Gant? The nearest town, perhaps? To the home of a kinsman?"

She shook her head and gazed away from him, out

from the trees and back the way they'd come. A faint frisson of alarm passed through him. He had no time—or indeed patience—for being saddled with a woman, no matter how intriguing.

"Perhaps," he suggested, "once passions back there die down, you can return home."

"You suppose so? I do not. I have seen the last of wondrous Slurt."

"Mistress Gant, I cannot take you on with me, at least not far. I am charged with a matter of great importance and cannot allow myself to be delayed."

"May I ask whence you are bound?"

"I ride first to the north of Aberdeen, where I must deliver grave tidings."

Her eyes widened. "So far? Please, Sir Malcolm, take me with you. I will ask no more."

Might there be a place at Crag Corvan for another servant? Would his father care if he attached this woman to the household? He did not suppose he could abandon her here along the road or see her driven back into danger.

He gave her a hard stare. "I ha' but one question for you, mistress: are you a witch? The truth of it now, for I've no time to become mired in further trouble."

She widened her eyes in a braw show of innocence. "Why, Sir Malcolm, do I look like a witch?"

Chapter Five

Tansy awoke from a dream filled with fire and pain. So real had it seemed—so vital—she lay for a moment even after she opened her eyes onto the soft darkness, her heart pounding in her ears.

There—there—was the fire, mere embers left now of the comforting blaze Sir Malcolm had built after nightfall. There, beyond the hillock behind which they'd sheltered, a sea of stars spread wide across the sky. Dawn had not yet arrived, though she sensed it would soon.

Ah, God, such a dream! She'd been chained in a dark place with the memory of pain writhing through her body and the promise of more to come. The screams of others echoed in her ears, and her own lodged in her throat. It must be a foreshadowing of what would have awaited her at the hands of the Commission.

A shudder passed through her, long and powerful. But for the grace of Sir Malcolm Montgomery...

Where was he? Had he deserted her here beside the lonely road north and moved on? He'd insisted she take the single blanket he possessed and—aye—had been sitting up beside the fire when she fell asleep. Not there now.

She pushed herself upright and surveyed the camp site. Sir Malcolm lay stretched, without benefit of blanket or pillow, upon the hard ground at the far side of the fire.

Fast asleep.

A score of thoughts tumbled through Tansy's mind. She could weave a wee spell, push him a bit deeper into slumber and make sure he stayed there. She could then help herself to everything he owned—that fine horse, the supplies strapped to the saddle, all worth a bit of coin. She would not dare steal the dagger in his belt or the great sword even now laid within reach of his hand, or any gold or silver he might have secreted about him. But she could make off with the rest of it and go to seek her fortune, no longer answerable to anyone, free to be the woman she was.

Usually, she resisted the urge to use the power that slept within her, or to weave any spells at all beyond mere suggestions that encouraged folk to do what she wished. She might magic Ossian to meet her in the dark lane behind the smithy, Ranna to step into a puddle and ruin the new slippers of which she was so proud. Now the ability came to her all too readily, tingled in her fingertips and her mind.

Dangerous.

She'd always known it to be so, even before she heard of the Royal Commission. Did she not have her mother's example before her? As well as the dark specter of what had happened at the crossroads.

Another shudder wracked her body. Perhaps best to just creep away with what she could carry before he woke, and leave magic out of it.

She stirred and started scrambling to her feet. The knight sat up also, as if connected to her by reins. By the powers! Had he but pretended to sleep?

He moved now like a shadow of himself, smooth enough to be supernatural. They stared at one another across the orange embers, and Tansy's pulse jagged.

"What is it, mistress?" he asked, his voice husky in the gloom. "What do you need?"

A good question, and one that had haunted Tansy most her life. For she had a need always burning inside, the nameless desire she thought could be answered by Ossian's company or Ranna's humiliation. Now she wondered fleetingly if even marriage with Ossian would have satisfied her.

She gestured wordlessly to the dark land beyond the fire. "I need to relieve mysel'."

He grunted. "Return swiftly."

He got to his feet even as she finished rising, the sword coming almost magically into his hand. Surely he did not mean to accompany her? But no; he kicked the fire into life. Sparks flew up like the bright dust from a spell.

Tansy slipped off into the darkness, biting her lip in consternation. Having done her business among the fronds of bracken, she came back to find him pacing like a restless wolf.

Ah, what approach to take with this man? Back in Slurt she knew everyone and could predict their reactions at most times. This man, with his dark face and shuttered eyes, made her uneasy precisely because she could not read him.

Yet she did not doubt there must be a way to handle him; experience told her most anyone could be handled.

She sank back down onto the blanket and said, "I am that sorry to have disturbed your sleep, Sir

Malcolm. You maun be gey weary."

"We will need to be on our way soon, by any road." He fed the fire, which leaped up. A strange feeling stirred within Tansy, in response. Such a handsome man, in his dark, compelling way. Dangerous as the predator he resembled.

"Will you break your fast?" he asked.

"Aye." She waited while he dug in the pack, and accepted the hunk of bread he passed into her hand. "It is good of you to share."

No response to that. He sat back down on the far side of the fire and lapsed into his brooding silence. Tansy concentrated on choking down the dry bannock, which stuck in her throat.

Not very good; Bessie baked far better. Surely she could not be longing for home, all because of a bit of bannock?

Yet she remembered the distress in Bessie's face, distress on her behalf, and her stomach grew tight. Would she ever see her family again? For most her life she'd felt like a cuckoo in the wrong nest. She should be grateful to get away.

To distract herself from her thoughts, she asked her companion, "Why do you ride to Aberdeen, Sir Knight?"

"My home is nearby. I take to my father tidings of one dear to us both."

A woman? Tansy wondered why the idea bothered her. This man's business remained his own.

"Have you been awa' on a quest?"

"I ha' been awa' in France, fighting at my father's behest. With my brother."

"Och, I see." And had the brother died in some

battle? Did that make up the burden he carried home? No wonder he appeared so grim. "Did he perish, your brother?"

"Worse." For a moment Tansy believed he would say no more. And why should he? Surely she made a poor confidante for such a man as this. Yet he choked down a bite of bannock and went on, "No sooner had we set foot in Scotland than we were waylaid and attacked. My brother, Mercien, is now the prisoner of our enemy."

For an instant Tansy could feel his pain—bright and immediate—as if it were her own. Darkness, fire— all too much like her terrible dream.

She gasped in reaction. "How did you escape?"

He slanted a look at her. "I did no'. Our captor has merely released me now in order that I might ransom my brother. By doing the untenable."

"Which is?"

"I dare not speak of it. And I did not figure on rescuing a witch at the crossroads. That is, if you do be a witch."

"I have told you I am not."

"You ha' told me so, aye, but I will be cursed if I know whether to believe it. Since I am sworn to uphold the weak and helpless, I will take you wi' me to Crag Corvan and find you a place there. But you maun understand I ha' no time to embroil mysel' in your troubles."

"Aye, Sir Knight. I am grateful for what you ha' done." Tansy squirmed; she hated being deemed either weak or helpless. Yet his perception of her as being so may have saved her life.

He said slowly into the darkness, "I could no' see

an innocent woman go into captivity and the kind o' questioning that would ha' followed it. The country has gone mad wi' this persecution o' witches. Even in France we heard of it."

"'Tis said the King himsel' is at the root of it. Will I be safe at this place, Crag Corvan?"

"I hope so. But for the love o' God, do no' go telling folk there what has befallen you or of what you were accused. I ha' no wish to bring more grief down upon my home and family."

"Have you a large family, Sir Malcolm?"

"Not so many left now. There were eight of us, once. My elder brother died, as did a wee sister last autumn with the sickness in her chest. Three other sisters are wed and awa'. Every loss and parting has taken a bit o' my father's heart. I do no' ken what the news I bring will do to him."

Tansy experienced an unwanted stir of sympathy. Usually most of her concern centered on herself—pity, longing, indignation.

Now she felt what this man felt and fell respectfully silent.

A cool wind sighed over the land. Far to the east, a tinge of pink appeared on the horizon.

"I will do my best, Sir Knight, to keep from bringing you any further grief. May I ask a question?"

"Ask, lass."

"Why did your captor let you free but continue to hold your brother?"

Sir Malcolm laughed harshly. "He knows if he holds Mercien, he continues to keep a hold on me. I dread Mercien's pain more than my own."

How awful. Tansy's emotions stirred still more

powerfully, like a deep river in her breast. "Were you tortured?"

Again, she thought he'd refrain from answering. He bowed his dark head before he said, "Och, aye. Worse than that, Master Latham of Ballan made certain I could hear Mercien being tortured."

"Who is this man—Master Latham of Ballan? And why—how—did he capture you?"

"You have never heard of him?"

Tansy shook her head.

"Surprising, as he is a man of some renown. Perhaps Dun Ballan is merely too far from Slurt."

She shifted on her blanket and tucked her bare feet beneath her. "Slurt is too far from everywhere." Save, perhaps, the Royal Commission.

"He is naught but a bandit who seized his holdings through devious dealings and violence. As a young man, he murdered his own father to attain his present position. He hates my family because we challenged his right to those holdings. That was before Mercien and I, with a stout company of men, were sent to France by order of the King."

Tansy said nothing. It felt as if Sir Malcolm spoke to himself rather than her; she dared not interrupt.

"I wonder now if that did not also come about at Latham's urging. The campaign in France proved disastrous; we lost all our men but two, and they had to be left behind because of their wounds. Mercien and I landed at Dundee alone. We took the road north, only to fall under attack. The attackers knew when we would make port, and were lying in wait. We ne'er had a chance."

An ill tale indeed. From clear across the fire, Tansy

could feel his frustration and grief. And she could feel anger, well banked.

"You were bound for home?"

"We were, and never made it. We spent more than a fortnight in Latham's dungeons—to speak truth, I lost count of the days. One does, mired in darkness."

Tansy thought again of the Royal Commission. Such might have been her dismal fate.

"And," Malcolm went on softly, "Mercien there still."

"Do you know how he fared when you left? What—what his condition may be?"

"Latham made sure to hold us in separate cells so we could provide one another no comfort or encouragement. He also made sure I heard each time Mercien went under torture."

"He is a monster, this Latham."

"You ha' no idea, mistress."

"And—and your condition, Sir Malcolm? You were tortured also."

He shifted uneasily. "Aye but not so extensively as Mercien. Latham gave me but a taste of what he handed out to my brother, so I would be sure to understand what Mercien endured. He always knew Mercien to be his most potent weapon against me. And does yet."

"Should you not be bound for the King to make complaint? As one of his knights…" She might not know much, but she understood it for an honored place in the eyes of the monarch.

Another rough laugh escaped Malcolm's lips. "The King? Latham is one of his closest friends, part of his inner circle. He will no' hear aught against him."

Tansy's eyes widened. "Then what will you do?"

Malcolm stared at her hard across the embers. "First I maun speak wi' my father. And then, Mistress Tansy Bellrose, I fear I maun tame my conscience."

Chapter Six

Malcolm bent a look on the woman who rode so close on the saddle, in front of him. During the last three days he'd become accustomed to having her there—the feel and scent of her, the constant awareness. For a peasant lass from an isolated clachan, she made a surprisingly good companion, lively, clever, and always willing to listen. In fact, she soaked up whatever he chose to tell her the way dry bread sops up wine.

As a consequence, he might have confided more than he should. After his harrowing experience at Dun Ballan, words seemed to tumble from him. Moreover, he missed Mercien's company. The two of them had tended to chat effortlessly when they traveled, as if of one mind.

Curious, but he felt of one mind with this lass also. Odd that he'd find a connection with someone he'd stumbled across by chance, a woman so different from himself. Yet half the time he could sense the thoughts moving in that black head of hers, and twice she'd roused him from deep and evil dreams in the night, with soft words.

And he sensed a restlessness in her that matched his own.

Now he wondered what she'd make of Crag Corvan. He loved the place with a deep and unwavering affection that, like his attachment to his father, followed him everywhere he went in the world—a tether, an anchor drawing him always home. An ancient settlement claimed by his Montgomery ancestors and theirs before them far into the mists of antiquity, it had been built around a stone tower that kept watch over the North Atlantic. The pile of rock might not look like much at first glance. But it sheltered Malcolm's heart.

"There," he whispered to Mistress Tansy Bellrose, "now you will see."

Time for no more. His weary horse breached the rise, and Mistress Tansy gave a satisfying gasp.

"Och, 'tis a jewel of a place. We go there?"

"Aye."

She turned on her perch to look at him. So near did she ride in his arms, her black hair brushed his chin. It felt like silk.

"You did no' say 'twas set beside the ocean. I ha' always wanted to live within sight of the sea."

"'Tis an ancient stronghold, this. Granted to my ancestors back in the time of Robert the Bruce, the original fortress has been here much longer. But as you can see, 'tis not so much by the sea but above it—there is no easy way down."

"You must be so glad to be home."

He was—a hard knot unfurled in his chest, affording him a measure of ease. At the same time, dread tightened his stomach. He brought ill news to his father, news he did not look forward to imparting.

"Aye," he said and chucked to the horse, to get him moving again. Rest soon, he promised the valiant beast. And a new life for the lass he'd brought.

As if reading his mind once more, she asked, "Sir Malcolm, what will my place be, here?"

A good question. Having now made her acquaintance, he could not imagine her suited to becoming a good servant. Too volatile, too filled with energy and ideas. Yet that would most likely be her fate.

Still, throwing her into the kitchen would be like tossing a fox among hens. Could she cook? Sew? Make cheese?

He grunted and said nothing. These many days, his body had argued hard about what he'd like to do with her. He'd entertained wild imaginings of her in his bed, warm and smelling of thyme as she did, and beyond willing. Not that she'd given him any indication she desired him, beyond an occasional look from those uncanny eyes.

He maun put such thoughts away from him. Did he not have enough over which to worry?

"Sir Malcolm?" she persisted. He'd learned she did not give up easily when pursuing what she wanted to know.

"I shall ask my father to place you where you can do the most good. What skills do you possess?"

"I am right clever with herbs and medicines. And I brew the best heather ale in all Scotland."

"Formidable skills. Our brewer is called Angus. I am no' certain he will welcome anyone interfering in his affairs, specially a lass. And our physician, Brother Matthew works alone in the dispensary."

"No' any more," she said smugly.

He laughed. "Well, we shall see."

She shot him another look over her shoulder, from so close he might have numbered her eyelashes had he wished. "One word of warning, Sir Knight: I am of no use in the kitchen. No point stationing me there."

He quirked an eyebrow. "Better, surely, than in the hands of the Commission?"

"Aye, but 'twould be a close thing."

****

No mistaking the man who embraced Malcolm Montgomery for anyone but his father. Sir Malcolm, as Tansy could see, was the spit of his sire, and gazing at Master Murgo, she fancied she beheld Malcolm in a score of years.

A handsome man and no mistake, though with a liberal helping of silver in his dark hair and a face scored, no doubt, by both living and pain. He and Sir Malcolm were nearly of a height and similarly built. Nor could she mistake the affection and relief with which Master Murgo clasped his son to him.

Yet a glad homecoming it proved not. Sir Malcolm soon drew away from Master Murgo's grasp far enough to speak. "Father…"

"Where is Mercien?" Master Murgo's face grew suddenly grim. "Never say he is lost! You sent word from France telling us you would both soon return home."

"Father, we maun speak together. The news is no' good."

"Where is your brother?"

"At Dun Ballan, a prisoner of Donald Latham. But…"

"You do no' say! That bastard." Master Murgo glanced round at the others gathered for this homecoming, including Malcolm's young brother and sister, both of whom listened avidly. "You are right— we maun speak. In my study. Nellie, bring the whisky."

41

Master Murgo's dark gaze fell on Tansy. "But who is this?" He gave his son a sharp look. "You did no' return to my household with some Frankish strumpet?"

Tansy stiffened indignantly. Was that how she appeared, like a foreign tart? And was Malcolm in the habit of keeping such company? She did not like the prospect, though to be sure, she had no claim upon him.

"This is Mistress Tansy Gant. I did offer her my assistance, Father, in order to remove her from peril. She needs refuge for a time."

"Mistress Tansy Bellrose Gant," Tansy elucidated, dropping a rough representation of a curtsy. They did not have much time for such niceties in Slurt. That didn't mean she could not rise to the occasion.

Master Murgo waved a hand. "Take her to the kitchens and see her fed. Everyone else, please leave mysel' and my son to speak together."

Tansy felt a touch on her arm. "Come," said a girl standing beside her. "Awa' as the master says."

Tansy followed with unwonted obedience, though she did hold back one instant in an attempt to catch Sir Malcolm's eye. Wholly engaged with his father, he spared her not so much as a glance.

Would he give her another thought? Or had she vanished from his mind?

She supposed she should be grateful either way. Had he not happened upon the crossroads when he did, where might she be now?

Her companion gave her a curious look. "Master Malcolm has ne'er before done this."

"Done what?"

"Brought home a servant."

"I am no' his servant," Tansy said, with some

umbrage.

"Nay? What be ye, then?"

A good question. Tansy looked at her companion, a lass of no more than fifteen or so, with hair the color of straw and an unusually pale complexion. She appeared a bit like those white spiders that sometimes clung to the rafters in the loft back home. Did she never see the light of day?

"I am Noreen, and I start the fires."

"Eh?" Tansy uttered, startled.

The girl with the straw-colored hair seemed proud of it. "I am up betimes and trusted to go from room ta' room, to see the fires laid and kindled so the important folk in the house are warm when they wake."

Somehow, Tansy kept from sneering. "When is 'betimes'?"

"Och, I rise well before first light."

"You are up creeping about this place in the dark and cold just so others can lie in comfort?"

"And arise in comfort," Noreen added happily. "'Tis a gey important task, so Mistress Dinmore says."

"Who is Mistress Dinmore?"

"She is in charge of us all, even in charge of you."

"I tell you, I am no servant."

"Aye, but you maun be, if you wish to stay. Everyone here does work, frae the high to the low."

"The high?" This time Tansy did sneer. "You say the masters here work?"

"Aye—hardest of all, Master Murgo running this great place and Masters Malcolm and Mercien fighting the King's battles. 'Tis an honor, just, to serve such men."

Well, Tansy thought, and that remained to be seen.

Chapter Seven

"'Tis grave news, grave news indeed," Murgo groaned. Seated in his great carven chair in the study, he seemed to have sunk in upon himself, all the lines that scored his face leaping into high relief.

Malcolm hated seeing that look on his father's face. Moreover, he hated being the bearer of news that put it there.

The sickness that roiled in his gut every time he so much as thought of Mercien, still languishing in Latham's dungeon, rose once again.

He loved his father with unqualified devotion and had watched him take blow after blow these past years—the loss of Malcolm's beloved mother. The deaths of two sons, Malcolm's brothers. The turning of his fortunes and the harshness of his king's actions against him.

And for the first time, to Malcolm, his father appeared old. This news of Mercien's imprisonment had gutted him. Murgo could not endure yet another loss.

What if he succumbed to grief? Malcolm could not fathom the loss of his father. But the terms he had laid forth over the past hour—the same with which Latham had presented him before he left Dun Ballan—were not likely to ease Murgo's mind.

Murgo lifted stunned eyes to meet Malcolm's.

"This is a hard thing to countenance. Yet your brother must be saved. How will you go forward?"

Malcolm's heart thudded within him. He'd traveled the long weary miles home from Dun Ballan longing only to place this terrible burden in his father's hands and ask the question, "We canna' possibly do as Latham has demanded—Father, what shall we do?" Now this man, upon whose wisdom he'd always relied, left it squarely with him.

He shook his head. "There must be options. We might appeal to the King—"

Murgo grunted and got to his feet, moving like a man in pain. "And would His Majesty listen to aught we might say?"

There was the question. As he'd told Tansy Bellrose on the trail, Latham lay in the King's pocket. "Surely he would ha' to hear a petition for wrongful imprisonment."

"And how long would that take? Weeks? Months? How long can your brother endure in that bastard Latham's hands?"

Malcolm made no reply, but the sickness inside him redoubled. He watched his father take a restless step around the chamber before pausing to gaze into Malcolm's face.

"I canna' lose another son."

"Mercien is strong."

"But not invincible."

"No man is invincible, Father." Flesh, as Malcolm well knew, could be damaged and endurance broken. Only loyalty lasted—and perhaps love.

"Malcolm." Murgo laid a heavy hand on his son's shoulder. "Tell me what you underwent at Latham's hands. Show me your wounds that I may learn from them and so measure Mercien's agony."

Without question, for he had always obeyed this man, Malcolm shed his weapons, laying them with a clatter on the stone floor. He shucked his leather jerkin and the tunic beneath, stripped his body one garment at a time, until he stood clad only in kilt and leggings. He spread his arms in an eloquent gesture and met his father's gaze.

"By God! By God," Murgo breathed. He muttered something more, half under his breath, in Gaelic, words Malcolm had not heard since his youth—imprecations to a deity far older than the Christian God. "What did that? Fire?"

"Hot irons." Malcolm could say no more. His jaw quivered, and for one terrible instant he feared he would break. He hauled on his stoicism, the same that had got him through the terrible moments when iron met flesh.

"And your brother—Mercien—endures this yet?"

Far worse. But Malcolm would not admit that to this stricken man who had once represented all he knew of strength.

He spoke only one word through clenched teeth. "Aye."

"My son! My son—you maun win him free." Murgo captured both Malcolm's shoulders between hard hands. "Whatever it takes."

"Latham made it clear he will accept but a single ransom in exchange for Mercien."

"Catha."

"By God, Father, I do no' think I can do it." Now Malcolm pulled away from his father and took a restless turn about the room. "Her father was your

friend. She has almost no protection in the world."
Mercien loves her.

Malcolm knew that for truth, the way he knew the color of his brother's eyes and what might prompt his smile. Catha was part of Mercien, blood and bone. All the while they fought together in France, Mercien had dreamed of her and prayed she would not accept the hand of another before he reached home again.

"Mercien," he said with certainty, "would rather perish in that dungeon than see Catha in the hands o' that monster."

"I do no' doubt it," Murgo agreed heavily. "Your brother is a man of honor and courage. But Malcolm, I would not rather see it. I ha' already lost two sons." Murgo hesitated one painful moment. "I impugn you to meet Latham's terms and win your brother free."

Now Malcolm turned on his father. "You would have me abduct an innocent woman, like a thief or a highwayman, and turn her over to that black-hearted *skagan*? You ken full well he only wants her lands. She has held out this long while—"

"I ken that fine, aye."

"And you know how Latham treats his women. There was that scandal wi' young Lacey MacMaster. Even the King got involved then."

Murgo wheeled and shouted, "I wish the young woman no harm, but we are speaking o' your brother's life! I ken he has feelings for Catha—"

Both Mercien and Malcolm had feelings for her, truth be told. Catha, with her strawberry-blonde curls, rose-petal complexion, and impish smile, had long held a place in Malcolm's heart also. Wed and widowed as a girl of fifteen, she'd sworn to accept no other husband.

But since her father's death last winter, she was a prize well sought.

Including by Donald Latham of Dun Ballan. Though Latham had not come out and said so, Malcolm had the distinct impression he'd presented his suit to Catha and been spurned. Latham was no man to accept refusal kindly, and his lands marched beside those of Catha's father.

Malcolm wondered why Latham did not merely seize Catha himself. Quite plainly the man had no scruples. Did he think taking a woman by violence would cause her to harden her heart against him? Far better to force the deed upon a man she'd trusted all her life—a childhood friend. Yet once delivered, Latham needs must force the lass into marriage. Malcolm did not see how Latham could win.

Nor how he could.

"I truly believe, Father, that given the choice, Mercien would sacrifice himself for Catha's well-being."

Murgo howled, "He is no' being given the choice. Now, son, will ye do my bidding or no'?"

Pain speared Malcolm's heart. "Da," he said. He had not used that name for this man since the age of eight, but he needed now to reach his father's heart. "You ha' no idea what it cost me to leave Mercien there and ride awa'. I ha' looked after him all his life." Three years older than his brother, he'd always felt protective. "I believe Latham, understanding the relationship between us, used that against me. Despite that, I beg you not to ask this task of me. Catha MacGunn trusts me."

"As do I." Flint had entered Murgo's eyes. "In this

life, son, we maun sometimes do distasteful things. Go and see your wounds tended. But be prepared to leave here as soon as ever you can. Each moment you delay costs your brother in agony."

Malcolm made one last attempt. "We might attempt an appeal to the King—"

"The King has gone mad, pursuing witches all over the country."

That made Malcolm spare a thought for the fey lass he'd brought back with him. Where was she now? Disappeared into the bowels of the keep, destined for servitude?

Somehow he could not see Tansy Gant yoked into service. Tansy *Bellrose* Gant. But he had little time to concern himself with her now, witch or no. And he had half a conviction she just might be a witch after all.

"Do as I ask, son. Act howe'er you must to free your brother and bring him home."

Malcolm nodded heavily. "Aye, Father."

"And go wi' God."

Ah, one thing Malcolm knew for certain—God had no part in this.

Chapter Eight

"Out! Out of my kitchen."

The head cook of Crag Corvan, in a state of high dudgeon, glared down her nose at Tansy. At Tansy's side, poor wee Noreen cowered, looking as if she expected a beating from the huge, glowering behemoth.

Which, Tansy decided, would occur over her dead body. Who did this florid woman with the loud voice and sweaty armpits think she was? Well, head of the place, obviously. That did not make her Queen, and Tansy had always abhorred bullying of any kind.

Ah—surely no place here for her, then. She experienced a stir of disappointment. At first when Noreen brought her in, she'd found the kitchen pleasant—warm, and redolent with the scent of roasting meat and good baking. She'd been seated at a table and fed her fill. Before long, even her feet felt warm.

Then the cook—Mistress Dee—had descended upon her, waving pots and ladles, making demands.

"Ye've had yer fill," she roared. "Now get your scrawny arse to moving and prove yer worth."

Tansy leaped to her feet, Noreen, who'd remained to keep her company, popping up beside her, only to find Mistress Dee still towering over her. She cocked back her head in order to meet the woman's furious eyes.

"I am no scullery maid," she retorted. "While I am

willing to work for my supper, 'twill be work worthy of me or none at all."

Mistress Dee fisted her hands on her hips. "High and mighty, is it? And you wi'out the shoes for your feet. Peasant! I should be afraid, on second thought, to let the likes o' ye touch our good pots and kettles."

"I am no peasant, but an educated woman who can write her own name. Can you?" Tansy challenged. Not a wise ploy on her part, for most the denizens of the kitchen now stood watching, and Mistress Dee's face turned an even brighter shade of red.

"And why would an honest woman like mysel' need to write her name? Or a gypsy like you, for all that. If you wish to eat another crumb in this house, you will do as you're bidden. Noreen," she bent a prodigious frown on Tansy's companion, "run and bring Mistress Dinmore."

The housekeeper. Aye, well, Tansy did not fear her, either. As soon as Noreen scampered off, she reached for the slender threads of magic that lay within. Should she weave them into a spell and blow this old harridan off her feet? Or would that cause more trouble than it was worth, and perhaps get her cast out of here…

Ah, but she wanted to see Sir Malcolm again.

Since he'd come to mind, she used his name without compunction. "Sir Malcolm Montgomery, who did bring me here, promised I would be given to work with Angus the brewer, seeing as how I brew the best heather ale in Scotland or the isles."

"Is that so?" Mistress Dee's eyes bulged.

"It is. Just ask him, if you do no' believe me."

"Call Master Malcolm awa' from his important

business to ask him about a scrap o' a lass such as yoursel'? We shall rather see what Mistress Dinmore has to say."

She reached out and pinched Tansy's shoulder between fingers like fireplace tongs, as if Tansy meant to try and escape, which she did not. The strands of magic inside Tansy burned and begged to be used. Tansy's not-so-well-hidden malicious streak came to the fore.

"Do you like to drink ale, Mistress Dee? If so, I should think you would ponder most carefully how you treat me—since I shall soon have access to every sip that passes your lips."

Mistress Dee screeched and let go of her. Just then the housekeeper, trailed by tiny Noreen, sailed into the kitchen.

"Now then, what is all this fuss? Mistress Dee, this is your domain—can you not run it wi'out my assistance?"

"'Tis this—this elven creature that has been thrust upon me. She does no' want to take orders and thinks she can choose the tasks that will earn her bread."

Mistress Dinmore, tall and thin as Mistress Dee was wide and beefy, stared down her nose at Tansy in a haughty fashion. "What would you have her do?"

"Scrub the pots, like any newcomer to this kitchen. But she says she's been promised—by Master Malcolm, no less—a place in the brew house. And she threatened to poison me."

"I did nothing o' the kind. 'Twas your own evil mind made you think so."

Mistress Dinmore struck Tansy a stinging blow across the face, so quick Tansy had no time to duck, and so hard it swayed her on her feet. No one in the kitchen so much as gasped, which branded it a common enough occurrence.

But rage suffused Tansy. Kindhearted Bessie had never struck her, and the most she'd ever received from her Da was a half-hearted swat with no intent to hurt behind it.

She stood with her cheek flaming, looking at the housekeeper from eyes that suddenly felt utterly cold. The threads inside her came together of their own accord in a pattern both simple and dangerous.

Still staring at Mrs. Dinmore, she tugged on one of those threads.

On the far side of the kitchen, a pot overturned, spewing its full complement of mush across a table. The flood hit a tall container, which promptly toppled over also, knocking into a pile of turnips, which broke loose and tumbled to the floor, where they rolled like a series of small boulders, making several kitchen maids squeak.

One of the lasses, leaping aside, bumped into a pot, which toppled into the fire, dumping a roast all trussed and seasoned, and starting another flood of gravy, that made the fire belch smoke. On and on the rolling chain of destruction came, accompanied by sharp rattles and clangs, exclamations, and bodies moving out of the way with alacrity, straight across the kitchen toward them, until at last Mistress Dinmore had to break eye contact with Tansy and take a horrified look.

By now, Mistress Dee was jumping up and down from one foot to the other, exclaiming in disbelieving dismay, "My kitchen! My kitchen! Get her out!"

Mistress Dinmore hissed like a kettle on the boil.

She turned to Noreen who stood by, cringing.

"Take her to the brewer's hut. Who am I to disagree with Master Malcolm?"

****

Malcolm grunted and closed his eyes as the dispenser, Matthew, smeared salve on the last of his wounds. Matthew, though he had once worked with the monks at Iona, could not be praised for his warm manner or gentle touch, and this ordeal had taken what seemed an age. At least Matthew—normally dismayingly inclined to chatter—had been struck dumb by the number and nature of Malcolm's wounds.

Now the tiny space, redolent with the scents of herbs and poultices, lured Malcolm toward sleep. Stretched on the pallet wearing nothing but his kilt, he watched the last of the light fade outside, his body wracked by exhaustion. Indeed, the only thing that kept him from sleep was Matthew's heavy hand.

They both heard the commotion from a long way off. Raised voices and the clatter of feet along the passageway outside caused Malcolm to open his eyes and the dispenser to lift shaggy brows.

"By the holy saints…" Matthew began.

Before he could complete the thought, Angus the brewer burst into the room. Large and obviously annoyed, wearing a stained smock that showed he'd been working, Angus towed a second figure behind him, one Malcolm recognized all too readily.

She looked small and disgruntled, her arm caught in the brewer's grip, yet far from cowed. Rather, her pale eyes burned with an expression that had Malcolm sitting up on the pallet, a curse escaping his lips.

Tansy's eyes widened when she beheld him, and a

new expression bloomed there. Her gaze skipped over his skin, touching him everywhere—on each burn and festering sore—in a manner far less concerned than assessing. Malcolm felt something stir in the back of his mind, a response to the emotions inside her, as well as a spear of heat lower down. For she looked at him the way a woman looked at a man she desired.

"Master Malcolm!" Angus began unhappily. "You know me for a patient man."

Well, that might be an overstatement. Malcolm knew Angus to be fussy, particular about his craft, and often disagreeable. This appeared to be one of the latter times.

But he said evenly, "Aye, Master Angus, to be sure."

"Yet I will not put up wi' this." Angus released Tansy's arm, casting her off from him with sudden alacrity. "A scrap of a lass from nowhere, coming in to my brew house and supposing she can tell me how to improve my ale."

Malcolm bent a look upon Tansy. Black hair swirling around her, she appeared anything but abashed and repentant. In fact, Malcolm would be hard pressed to say when he'd seen anyone less abashed.

Her eyes, narrowed between long black lashes, met his. He felt that tickle at the back of his mind again.

He got to his feet. "What is the meaning of this?" he asked her directly.

But Angus answered, "She was foisted upon me by Mistress Dinmore, Mistress Dee having thrown her out of the kitchen. From what I hear, she destroyed that place. They could not get shed of her quickly enough."

Tansy tossed her head. "I am no scullery maid, nor

am I accustomed to taking orders from folk less intelligent than mysel'."

Disquiet stirred in Malcolm's heart. "Yet," he said sternly, "you must earn your way here. Everyone does."

Angus howled, "That is why they foisted her upon me. She claims to ha' a talent for brewing ale."

"I do ha' a talent for it. And Master Angus's brew could be improved. I ha' sampled it—"

"Wi'out my permission!"

"—and its flavor could only be enhanced by the judicial addition of—"

Malcolm felt his own eyes bulge. "Mistress Gant, Master Angus's ale is legendary here at Crag Corvan. I am certain no one wants it changed."

She sniffed. "That is merely because those here ha' become accustomed to an inferior brew."

Angus choked. "Upstart! Lass, I will have you know I ha' been brewing ale longer than you ha' been alive."

"And doing so poorly." Tansy tipped her head and considered. "Nay, I can no' say that. 'Tis no' the worst ale I ha' ever tasted, but no' so good as my own."

"Hold me back!" Angus roared to Matthew, who stood aghast. "Else I will wring her scrawny neck."

Matthew seized hold of the brewer's arm.

"Come now," said Malcolm, striving for reason. "I am sure the two o' you can come to terms. Mistress Gant, you maun accept Master Angus's authority if you are to work in the brew house."

"I will no' have her in the brew house. Send her back to the kitchens."

Malcolm thought of Mistress Dee, a mountainous woman who intimidated even him. "Perhaps not, if they ha' already tossed her out."

Tansy glanced around the dispensary. "I also have some knowledge of salves and potions. Mayhap I could do my duty here."

"Nay!" Matthew let go of Angus and waved his hands wildly. "I will not have her here if she is a disruptive influence. My patients need nurturing and calm."

Malcolm heaved a sigh. "Then pray tell me what I am to do with her."

Chapter Nine

"I do no' think 'tis wise for you to leave Crag Corvan so soon, before you regain your strength. And why are we bound back the way we came?"

Tansy had gotten a good look at the wounds Sir Malcolm wore beneath his clothing—had gotten a look at nearly all of him, in fact, and a proud eyeful it had been. She'd seen her share of near-naked men, including Ossian, whom she'd once considered an example of male perfection. She'd never imagined a man as beautiful as Malcolm Montgomery.

Pleasing in every regard, he was, from his broad shoulders, well-sculpted by muscle, to the rippled stomach and tantalizing trail of black hair that cleaved it. The very memory made her fingers tingle with the desire to touch. She wondered if she might seduce him. She wondered, a bit breathlessly, if she should.

At present, he most certainly entertained a foul mood, and had ever since they left Crag Corvan. Sour and dark, he brooded, saying almost nothing. She'd need to apply a good deal of persuasion, in order to learn his plans.

So, she would.

At least now she had her own mount—a pretty little mare—and had been fitted out with traveling supplies including shoes, stockings, and a fine, heavy cloak. She'd washed herself most carefully back at the keep and braided her hair neatly. She felt like quite the lady.

Malcolm shot her a dour look. "You've no need to understand. You will no' travel far wi' me."

Having made the pronouncement, he once more fell silent. Frustration arose and seized Tansy by the throat. She did not enjoy being thwarted. "We are no' going far?"

"I am, indeed. You are no'. 'Twould ha' been much easier to leave you at Crag Corvan, but you ha' made that impossible. I shall need to divert my path and deliver you to the household of a friend, instead." He bent a hard glare on her. "And none o' your disobedience, mind. I'll no' haul you wi' me all over Scotland."

"But—"

"I ha' not the time for it, nor the patience."

Indignation followed in the wake of Tansy's frustration. "I was more than willing to offer my services to your father's household. Can I help it if they refused me?"

"I fear, Mistress Gant, you ha' a woeful inability to accept direction."

"I might ha' been of great use in the dispensary. That foolish man would no' give me the opportunity. As for that, I could be of great use to you now, if you'd agree to take me wi' you."

"Impossible."

"Quite possible, and 'twould be a fine idea. Those wounds of yours will need tending, lest they rub raw beneath your clothing and turn poisonous."

"It does not matter."

"Of course it does. You ha' no' shared the details

o' your quest wi' me," she said cunningly, "save you maun attain the release o' your brother. I do ken you needs must stay well, if you are to succeed. I could no' help but notice the supplies that man, Matthew, gave you to bring along. I will be much better at using them than you will."

"I am no' taking you wi' me. Let that be an end to it."

Tansy fingered the strands of magic in her mind. Tempting, very tempting, to twist them together into a spell that would give him just a wee push and make him more agreeable to her wishes. Curious how back home in Slurt, despite her boredom, she'd mostly resisted using the ability that lodged within, save in giving Ossian a nudge from time to time or making Ranna spoil her fine appearance. When it came to this man, the urge seemed near constant.

She did not want him leaving her off somewhere along his way and going on to forget her. Nay, for she wanted to mean something to him.

That thought stood out in her mind. She surrounded it with a haze of magic—like light—and contemplated it.

Sir Malcolm glanced at her sharply, as if he heard the words in her mind. A bit more kindly he said, "I ha' told you I've a task to perform, one that could no' be more important. I canna' be held back."

"How d'ye ken I would hold ye back?"

He examined her, his dark gaze lingering on her hair before moving all the way to her newly shod toes.

"Call it instinct. You will. I just know it."

Tansy huffed. "How far to this place where you mean to get shed of me?"

"As I say, 'tis not far. I hoped we might reach there this evening, but we got too late a start. We shall ha' to lie over on our way."

Tansy bit her lip. Ah, then she had a chance yet to persuade him—and given the means of persuasion she had in mind, the dark of the night might serve her very well.

****

Weariness began weighing on Malcolm long before they paused for the night. He'd not yet regained his strength after those terrible days of captivity, and Mistress Tansy was right about one thing. The wounds beneath his clothing chafed maddeningly. Not at all in a happy frame of mind by the time he called a halt to their travels, he instructed her to help make camp in a copse of trees back off the road, and unloaded their supplies.

Night had already fallen, soft and dark. To Malcolm's surprise, Tansy set about her tasks without complaint. She gathered deadfall and built a cheerful little blaze before she unpacked the food and spread rugs near the fire, all while Malcolm tended the horses.

Before he'd finished, she had heated a mug of ale, which she passed into his grateful hands.

He drank deeply. "Ah, good. Thank you."

"Sit down," she ordered. "We will take somewhat to eat, and then I will ha' a look at those hurts o' yours."

He did not argue but sank onto one of the rugs and let the warmth of the fire soak into him.

He remembered the penetrating cold of Latham's dungeon and how he'd shuddered there, in his chains against the clammy wall. Suddenly his pleasure in the warm drink dissipated; how could he enjoy anything when Mercien remained there still? He lowered his cup.

Tansy seated herself close beside him. "What is it? Are you no' thirsty?"

"Nay."

"Hungry, then? I had these oatcakes fresh from the kitchen. I am surprised Mistress Dee gave them over; I expect she thought them meant for you."

"No matter. You eat them."

She bit into one with alacrity. Malcolm's stomach turned.

"So tell me how you mean to go about this braw task of yours. Perhaps I can help."

He glared at her. "Get that notion clear out o' your head. You will stay wi' my friend, Master Cunningham, and no fuss, mind."

She widened those pale eyes at him. "Me? Fuss?"

That made him smile grimly. "I begin to learn of you, Mistress Gant. You trail trouble in your wake."

"I do no'."

"Deny it as you will. Evidence argues to the contrary."

"That is unco' harsh. You scarce know me."

"Yet your fellow villagers found it necessary to tie you to a post, and no one at Crag Corvan would agree to keep you in his or her employ."

She tossed her head. "What makes you suppose your friend Cunningham will be any different?"

"I tell you what; you are to become a reformed woman, Mistress Gant. When I leave you wi' Master Cunningham, you will be docile, obedient, and accommodating in whatever tasks are assigned to you. Otherwise I will instruct him to cast you out on the street, to fare as you may."

She stared. "Well, then, I will just follow you on to wherever…"

"You will no'. I shall be long gone."

Her mouth grew hard and mutinous. She said nothing.

Malcolm gulped down more ale, even though the first mouthful had soured in his stomach. She crumbled her oatcake in her fingers.

At length she spoke. "So where are you bound?"

As if he would tell her that. 'Twas all he would need—this wench turning up at Castle Gunn whilst he endeavored to abduct his childhood friend.

"No' something you need to know, given it has naught to do wi' you. Now let us get some rest. I want to be awa' wi' the dawn."

"Not yet. I maun insist you tak' somewhat to eat."

"You insist?"

"Aye. And there are still your hurts to tend." She laid her food aside. "Best strip off your clothes."

"Eh?"

Their eyes met in the firelight. Suddenly Malcolm's breath froze in his lungs and his body tightened in a way he did not expect. Aye, he'd felt attracted to her all the while they rode the miles to Crag Corvan, sharing one saddle. But this was no' the time, and she could scarcely be a worse choice of woman.

Still, would she be willing? Here beside the fire— might he lose himself in her wildness, in the promise he saw in those bright eyes? Might it bring him some measure of relief?

Madness. She spoke only of tending his wounds. Did she not?

She leaned closer, and his heart pounded in his ears. He wanted her so much he could barely think.

Her lips parted. She meant to speak.

"In which pack will I find the bundle from the dispensary?"

Mind still frozen, he focused on her lips. How would she taste? Warm and sweet? Spicy and dangerous? Why did he long so to know?

'Twas like some measure of enchantment.

She smiled, a woman's smile, a cat's smile, and scrambled to her feet. "I will just look for it, shall I?"

As soon as she stepped away from him, the desire eased. Yet the remnants had him unfastening the front of his leather jerkin and unlacing the tunic beneath.

"Ah, here. This salve smells of comfrey and yarrow. 'Twill serve." She returned with the bundle in her hands, moving in that light way she had. Malcolm steeled himself for her touch.

She laid the bundle at his knee and untied it.

"Aye." He barely knew what he said. He watched through narrowed eyes as she dipped her fingers into the pot of Matthew's salve.

"Will ye remove your clothing, or shall I?"

Their eyes met for another blinding moment before Malcolm looked away, shrugged out of the jerkin, and eased the tunic over his head. She reached for his shoulder.

This had been a painful procedure when Matthew undertook it back at Crag Corvan. Now, before her fingers met his flesh, he felt a little whisper pass over his skin, the merest flicker of air. Where he expected pain, pleasure instead ensued.

"What was that? What did you just do?"

Concentrating on her task, black lashes lowered, she failed to answer. He seized her wrist. "Mistress Gant, did you just use magic on me?"

"I told you, I am no witch."

Doubt assailed Malcolm in a tumble. Davey Cunningham, a godly man, kept a Christian household. How could he foist this imp upon him?

"Aye," he muttered, "so you said." Was he a fool? By all that was holy, her own people had wanted to send her away to the Commission.

Before he could question her further, she observed, "These are gey ugly wounds, and no' mistake—inflicted over a number o' days. Do you wish to speak o' it?"

"'Tis no story for your ears, that."

"This is what the monster, the one you call Latham, did to you." Her fingers glided over his skin, spreading healing and leaving a flicker of arousal in their wake. Across one shoulder, down his neck, onto his chest, plowing a path through the hair, patches of which had been singed away. All at once he could no longer remember the pain.

Ah, God! Her touch felt like heaven.

Still he did not speak, and her eyes engaged his. "If your brother, Sir Mercien, has endured the like o' this, or worse, I do no' wonder that you worry for him. How do you mean to win him free, though? I am thinking 'twill be no easy task."

"Not easy at all, no." Suddenly Malcolm wanted to unburden himself to her, bleat out all his doubts like a child. He could not, he would not.

She whispered, like an invitation from the devil's lips, "Tell me all about it. 'Tis but the two o' us here, and no one else to listen. Wha' harm is it, to confide in me?"

Aye, but he could scarcely bear to put into words the terrible thing he had to do. He recalled the look in his father's eyes when Murgo bade him undertake the betrayal of Catha, a dear friend who trusted him. For Mercien's sake—naught existed now, save ransoming Mercien. No honor, no other loyalty, no attraction to this wee lass who knelt very nearly in his arms.

He shook his head, bitterly.

She went on speaking her words like a song. "I ken, me, wha' it is to lack a confidant. Back in Slurt, there was no one in whom I could confide. No one else like me. If there had been, I sometimes think it might ha' acted to reduce the mad impulses that so often rose to my head."

Aye, well, there was that. If he told Mistress Gant what he went to do, and she—with her questionable morals—found exception to it, might he not then need to think again?

He watched her fingers dip back into the jar, anticipating where they would next meet his flesh. He wanted to lie back and feel not only her fingers but her lips on him.

"I canna' leave Mercien in that place. Not at any cost."

"I quite see that, aye."

"My wounds are as naught to what he has endured. I maun free him." Sickness twisted Malcolm's gut again. How could he think of her touch, or anything else? "So you see I canna' let aught interfere."

"I see, aye." Her fingers moved again, brushing downward across the muscles of his abdomen. "But you canna' possibly expect to free him on your own."

"Aye, but I can, Mistress Gant—provided I make Latham the right payment."

Chapter Ten

Tansy stared at the grim edifice before which she and Sir Malcolm stood. Constructed of cold gray stone, its color matched the day, which had dawned with a sharp wind and the threat of rain.

She glanced at the man beside her. Following their conversation last night while she'd tended his wounds, they'd tried to sleep. She knew he had not succeeded—she'd heard him moving restlessly and guessed at the thoughts in his mind. It could not be pain from his hurts keeping him awake; she'd woven a wee spell to take that away—just a tiny one and certainly no harm in it.

As for her, she'd fallen into sleep at last only to experience a series of dreams, ones which she now understood: fire, darkness, and pain. A terrible place sharp with cold, flaring bright with agony. Before, she'd supposed she anticipated what awaited her at the hands of the Commission. Now she understood she must share Sir Malcolm's memories.

But how? And why? Was it because she'd woven that desperate spell at the crossroads, reached out and ensnared him? Did the threads of enchantment linger and somehow link them?

If they did, it seemed they would not keep him from abandoning her here in this terrible place with his friend, Cunningham.

How could she bear it?

Touching him last night had been agony of a different kind. She'd felt desire, aye, for Ossian, especially when she sought to influence him, and pleasure in his bonny appearance. Nothing like this.

And was she to watch this man ride out of her life?

She should have taken full advantage last night when she had the chance, insisted he remove his kilt and leggings, beneath which she knew very well he'd grown hard for her. His injuries extended there also— she had the excuse of needing to tend them. Something in his eyes had kept her from it.

Now she knew naught but regret.

Baldly she said, "I will never endure life in such a place as this."

He gave her a look of surprise. "But you ha' no' even seen inside…"

"I have no need to. I can feel it."

"Do no' be foolish, lass. I can afford to spend no more time on you."

"You maun go back to that place, in order to save your brother." She stared at him, and saw the flames and darkness of last night's dream. "What if you are captured once again?"

"'Tis naught to you, my fate."

"Is it no'?" She continued to gaze at him, wishing she could explain the connection between them. She might have snared him with a wee spell; it had caught her as well.

"Nay. Come."

A servant answered his rap at the door, a young girl in a neat gown and apron. Another—a lad—ran out to tend their horses. Before they gained the hall, a big, bluff man emerged from an inner room and greeted Sir

Malcolm heartily.

"Malcolm! How wonderful to see you. And an unexpected surprise! The last I heard, you and Mercien were still in France."

"Davey." Malcolm clasped Cunningham's hand heartily, and the man smiled.

"What brings you to us, my friend?"

Malcolm stole a look at Tansy. "Davey, I have a terrible great favor to ask."

****

"Will I see you again?" Tansy pushed the hair out of her eyes and gazed at the man who stood in front of her. All clad for leaving he was, with his leather armor covering all those sore wounds. He looked grave and purposeful; she could feel he'd gathered himself up with a stern hand, focused on what lay before him.

Not on her.

Suddenly she could not bear it. Not so much that he should dismiss her from his mind—for once she did not need to be the center of attention, and she'd glimpsed, now, that which rode him—but for him to leave her for weeks, or perhaps months, not knowing what might befall him. For her to imagine the worst, lurid scenes akin to those dreams of fire and darkness.

His gaze rested on her at last; the corners of his mouth, so tight, eased a bit.

"Perhaps, lass. Perhaps not."

She did not like the answer. Were she to accompany him, she might be able to help him in his quest, and ease his way, though he would never believe it so. She would at least know whether he lived or died.

"You will do well enough here, Tansy Bellrose Gant, if you keep obedient. Master Cunningham's wife

70

is a verra kind lady."

"She does seem so." Plain-faced and gentle-voiced, Mistress Cunningham did not appear the sort to shout at her servants. Ironically, she'd assigned Tansy the same duty poor wee Noreen had performed back at Crag Corvan—that of rising betimes to light the fires. Tansy would also help round the place where needed, scrubbing, fetching and carrying, and polishing Master Cunningham's boots to a high shine.

In return she would receive her keep and half a day off every fortnight.

"And Davey Cunningham is a good man. Do no' try him." Sir Malcolm hesitated. "Give me your word, now, before I leave. I would prefer to leave easy in my mind and knowing you well settled."

He cared. Because of the wee push she'd given him with her magic? Or another reason?

If he left her here, she'd never know, and it made her heart ache.

Tansy gazed into his eyes, searching. Deep as a moonless night they were, and nearly as fathomless.

"I promise I will no' grieve Master Cunningham." How could she, if she did not remain in his household? "Go with God and may the blessing of all the spirits, Sir Malcolm, keep you safe. And thank you. Thank you for saving my life. If I can ever repay that debt, I will."

"You can best repay it by staying here, keeping safe and being obedient."

So he might well say; she had her own ideas. Unlike any servant or much less a rescued waif, she reached up one hand and laid her fingers against his cheek. He blinked in surprise and froze like a hare before a fox.

She whispered words in the Gaelic, an old, old charm to bring him back again. And then, stretching on her toes, she replaced her fingers with her lips.

Delight—instant and forceful—made her dizzy, even as daring possessed her soul. He tasted just the way she'd imagined, felt as she'd imagined, too, the rough stubble on his face and the deep warmth. The threads of magic sleeping inside her stirred and unfurled without her volition.

Kiss me.

Did she think the command, or did he? No matter, for they moved together instinctively and at once. His gauntleted hands settled at her waist, hers crept around his neck, and their lips met.

It felt hot as fire, effortless as the magic inside her when it came, and sweeter than any spell. Och, no man should taste so good as this. 'Twas a woman's downfall, her saving and her condemnation. For a woman would toss away the sure promise of heaven for this.

It should have been a fleeting caress—a salute, a farewell, a mere brush of lips on lips. Instead it turned into hunger, and Tansy readily opened her mouth to his, opening her soul as well.

Kiss me.

Their tongues tangled, a thing she'd never imagined. Ossian did not kiss like this. He slobbered, aye, and sucked at her mouth, but did not woo or give. This became a wild dance, tongue with tongue, and Malcolm's flavor flooded into her, imparted itself, a thing she would never forget.

"Forgive me." He broke the kiss and, breathing raggedly, rested his forehead against hers.

Forgive him? She wanted to present all of herself to him—on a platter if need be.

"There is naught to forgive."

"That was far too bold of me, Tansy Bellrose Gant."

"It was divine."

He began to laugh softly. She'd never heard him laugh, and it delighted her to the bone.

"You know it was," she insisted.

"Minx. But I canna' deny it."

Do not deny me. Do not leave me here. Do not pull my heart up by the roots and go away. I will suffer anything to be with you.

The thoughts shocked her. Everything about this shocked her—she, who would have claimed she could not be shocked.

"Something sweet to carry awa' wi' me."

"Nay." She trapped his face between her hands, forcing him to meet her gaze. She wanted to kiss him again, so much she could scarcely breathe. "Take me wi' you."

"Mistress, Tansy, I canna'. Not where I go."

"Into danger."

"Aye."

"To this terrible, hard rescue."

"'Tis a tortuous path. A risky one."

"Let me come wi' you. I care not what happens to me after."

"Madness."

"It is meant. Sir Malcolm, ha' you never felt something is just meant?"

"I did no' rescue you at that crossroad just so you might endanger yoursel' again." Very gently he disengaged from her grasp. "Let me go."

Tansy stood gazing at him with rebellious eyes, her breath coming in gasps.

No, no, no.

He smiled sadly. "Take care, Mistress Gant. It will hearten me, thinking of you."

"Tansy Bellrose Gant," she corrected instinctively, but the words came only in a whisper and he heeded them not. Swiftly he strode away from her, away from the rear door of Master Cunningham's house to the place where his horse waited.

For an instant the bright morning darkened all around Tansy. She saw blackness and death.

"Come back—"

But her cry dissipated in the clatter of hooves on stone, and he rode from the courtyard with nary a backward glance.

Chapter Eleven

It must be enchantment; Malcolm could think of no other explanation. He should be focused completely on the difficult and morally fraught mission before him—abducting a woman he admired in order to ransom his brother. Instead he kept finding Tansy Bellrose Gant pushing her way into his thoughts: how she had felt in his arms, how she'd tasted. The sensation that rushed through him when she placed her hand against his cheek, like claiming, like recognition and desire all in one.

She must be an enchantress, to turn his thoughts so. That meant he'd likely liberated a witch from her just fate, at that crossroads. But how could such a fate—of pain and fear and forced confessions—possibly be just?

His heart told him it could not, just as it argued there must be more to Tansy Bellrose Gant than met the eye. She might well be able to enchant him with her kisses.

Just imagine how lying with her would feel.

He banished that thought from his mind, or tried to. Desire remained like a seed inside him, and he caught quick glimpses of things that had never happened: Mistress Tansy by firelight, naked and spread before him like a banquet. Mistress Tansy applying that clever tongue of hers to his skin. Her black hair loose and twined around them when they moved together in an exquisite storm of completion.

None of it had occurred; none ever would.

Curse it.

She must have used magic to make him want her so. He needed to think of Mercien. Of Catha and what he would say to her when he arrived at Castle Gunn.

Tansy, Tansy, Tansy. Her name whispered over and over in his mind. He saw her again, standing, gazing up at him, her eyes peering into his soul.

Best he was shed of her. Had they remained together, it would have progressed beyond kisses. He—noted for his superb control—would have broken like a weir before the floods. And he couldn't afford that, not now.

He called up Catha's countenance in his mind. How long had he loved her? Forever. How long had she loved Mercien? Just as long. Sold by her father as little more than a child, she'd escaped the cruel union upon her husband's death and chosen to come home, an heiress.

Malcolm had no doubt Latham wanted her wealth. Latham also wished, no doubt, to break her, for that was what Donald Latham did.

Could Malcolm hand her over to that fate? And what to tell his father, if he failed?

So caught up in thought was he, he almost missed it when his mount stumbled. So far, the beast had proved faultless, answering every demand, but now it slowed and began to limp.

Malcolm's heart sank. At the side of the road he pulled up and dismounted, speaking to the beast reassuringly.

The horse blew and rolled its eyes in distress,

favoring its left front hoof. An examination left blood on Malcolm's hands and chagrin in his heart. A sharp stone had worked its way deep into the foot, and the shoe welled with blood.

A disaster for a knight in any circumstances—for him, doubly so. He tried to remember a smith located nearby and failed. He would either need to dislodge the stone himself or turn and limp back to Donald's.

Twenty minutes' labor with his dirk left him sweating and the horse uncooperative. Unwilling to hurt the loyal beast, he'd just accepted the need to turn back when he heard another rider coming up behind.

Nay, two riders. Dared he hope they might be Christian souls willing to offer assistance?

He straightened just in time to see them round a curve in the road. Ah, but there was but one rider after all—the second animal came led by the first.

Recognition hit him like a blow to the gut—quick and hard. How could she have known what road he'd taken?

And had she come because he kept her at the forefront of his mind?

Mistress Gant drew up her mount—the little mare she'd ridden away from Crag Corvan—in the road and looked at him. She'd wrapped herself close in her cloak; very little of her countenance showed, just those uncanny eyes and a few stray wisps of black hair.

She flung her gaze at his disabled mount and seemed to ponder what to say, a first in their acquaintance.

Malcolm, having no such hesitance, barked, "What are you doing here? Did I no' bid you stay wi' Master Cunningham?"

"Aye." She cocked her head like a wee black bird. "But you ha' need of me. Did no' get very far wi'out me, did you?"

He grunted, near stupefied by the emotions that filled him: anger, amazement, and—if he were honest—a measure of relief. Mayhap, with her arrival, he would not have to turn back after all.

"How did you ken my horse was in trouble?" He narrowed his eyes. "Did you hex him so he'd pick up that stone?"

"Do no' be foolish," she bade with notable lack of respect. "I would do naught to harm that fine beast—or you. I am here to help."

"Aye, so. Give me your mare and lead my mount back to the Cunninghams'. Master Davey will see a blacksmith tends him."

She slid down from the back of the mare and approached Malcolm. "The mare will never carry your weight and that of all your gear."

"She will."

"'Twould be cruel. I will no' countenance it. You maun use this other mount I ha' fortuitously brought."

He bent a hard stare on her. "You will no'?" Indeed, and she took far too much upon herself. "Where did you get that other horse?"

"He is one of Master Cunningham's."

Malcolm went cold. "You stole him?" Aye, she would hang for sure.

"I did not. I secured his loan from Mistress Cunningham, who proved a most reasonable and supportive confidant. She said her husband would surely supply you with aught you might need if asked."

"But he was no' asked."

"He was not at home. And the situation seemed too dire for us to wait." Her tone turned petulant. "You might at least admit you are glad to see me."

He took a step toward her and attraction reached out like a snake to curl around him. By heaven, he never should have kissed her. Now the desire would not stay where it belonged.

"You ha' not said, Mistress Tansy, how you knew I would need another mount. You must have left shortly after I did, in order to follow so close."

"I left as soon as I could persuade Mistress Cunningham and prepare the horses. As for how I knew…" She paused and again contemplated her thoughts before going on. "I just did. It came to me all in a flash, the moment you rode away. Something would befall your mount—"

"Something you claim you did no' help to cause." He made his voice stern. "By enchantment."

"You accuse me of witchcraft?"

"Let us at least be honest wi' one another, Mistress Tansy. You are as your townsfolk named you."

"There is no harm in it. And I can be of great use to you."

He snorted. "Aye, you can." Before her eyes had a chance to light, he went on, "You will take my hobbled mount back to Master Cunningham's house, along with my thanks for the loan of this other."

She drew herself up. "I am coming with you."

"Mistress, we have already had this discussion."

"I owe you my service in return for rescuing me. Not your father or Mistress Cunningham. If you bring me along, I will be silent and biddable."

"Ha!"

"And I will no' interfere with your quest. But I will come. If you turn me awa' now, I shall merely follow as I ha' been doing."

Christ. What had he done to deserve her hung about his neck like an anchor? Rage crashed over him, swiftly followed by lust. If he brought her along, might he then have her here on the road, and assuage his desire before undertaking the impossible? Ah, such a temptation!

She stepped closer, and he caught her scent, which seemed to have infected him back at the Cunninghams', when he kissed her.

"What of my mount? Someone needs must take him back to Aberdeen."

She smiled a cat's smile, a cat with cream on its whiskers. She thought she'd won. "I can whisper a wee spell, one wi' no harm in it, and send him back safely to the Cunninghams. I promise no ill will befall him."

Aye, and she admitted what she was. Had she also whispered a wee spell pushing him to accept her?

"You make a lot of promises."

"And I keep them."

"Do you?" He challenged her with his gaze. "If I bring you along, Mistress Tansy Bellrose Gant, do you promise to place yourself in my hands? To be completely obedient? To do whatever I ask?"

Her tongue came out and wetted her lips. All at once he could taste her again, sharp and vital. He went hot and began to sweat.

If she agreed, he could always send her away later. After he'd had her, perhaps. She would be completely in his power—by her own volition.

She eyed him slowly from the top of his head

downward, lingering at a few places on the way. She drew a ragged breath.

"Aye, Master Knight. So I do promise."

Chapter Twelve

Soon. It must be soon. Tansy must have Sir Malcolm Montgomery for her own, or she would surely perish.

Dhe, and she had not expected him to ride so far, or for so long. They had sent the injured mount back, guarded by that wee spell, hours ago, though it felt like days. Since then, Tansy's mare had followed Master Cunningham's horse and Sir Malcolm had scarcely so much as spoken to her, even though she threw all her persuasion at his muscular back.

Now, with night coming on, her long wait surely must be at an end. For she tired of staring at the back of his black head and her body—overly sensitized by desire—could barely endure the touch of her own clothing.

They needed to shed their clothes, both of them, and complete this act that would ease her. Soon.

She knew he wanted it as much as she did. Desire streamed from him like scent, and his refusal to look at her meant nothing. She knew, too, he had quite likely allowed her to accompany him for just that single purpose; she'd seen the look in his dark eyes when he agreed. She did not mind that. Persuasion would be easier accomplished in his arms.

At that thought, she shivered like a woman with fever. And, in answer to her prayer, he at last drew up his mount.

Here? She looked about. No town or clachan, no inn. Just a barren stretch of road, and a few trees. But aye, it would serve. For here came the blessed moon, rising full and golden-bellied through the branches, and anywhere she might be alone with this man would be good enough.

Still without looking at her, he said, "We will lay over here tonight."

Aye, they would.

He dismounted and led his horse away into the trees. Tansy followed. There he asked her, "Will you gather wood for a fire as you did before? But for God's sake, do no' set the copse alight. I will tend the horses before we tak' some supper."

"We will both tend the horses."

He spun to look at her. "What's become of that obedience you promised?"

She shrugged. "No need to go mad wi' it. The two of us tending the horses will make the job quicker. And I ha' no need of a fire. Or food."

His gaze narrowed on her. Could he fail to understand?

To make things clearer, she stepped up to him. "I think you ken fine what I want."

The kiss exploded between them, hotter than any fire she could kindle, and she pressed her body to his, luxuriating in the sensation. Ah, this had she craved. This did she need: her mouth fused to his in answer to the unbearable ache of demand.

"Tansy." He broke the kiss and gasped her name. "Are you certain?"

"Is this no' the reason you brought me along? To

give you comfort. Succor. Pleasure."

"I will no' force you. Have you had a man before?"

She laughed. Aye, she'd lain with Ossian. That, she sensed, bore no relation to this.

"Malcolm." She gazed into his eyes and spoke his name in claiming. "I want this, only this. I want you, only you." She smiled. "I will prove most obedient."

Heat flared in his eyes, and he swore in what sounded like wonder. She'd intended to give him a little push from the magic simmering inside her. It would not be necessary. His hands shook as he began removing his clothing; his gaze burned on her as she unfastened her own garments.

Aye, and she'd never been so anxious to shed them. Not even with Ossian. That had been exciting, even daring. Now desire thrummed deep inside her, impossible to deny.

What would he think of her body? Small and willow slender, she made up in agility what she might lack in bosom. And he—aye, she'd glimpsed most of him back in the dispensary. Now, as his clothing came away, she saw his full magnificence. Long, muscular legs. That rippled stomach she'd glimpsed while tending his wounds. And—

Words failed her when she dropped her gaze. Thoughts failed her. She—who had never cared for anyone but herself—became aware of a strange desire to worship him.

"You are gey beautiful," she said.

He did not hear her. Wrapped in desire far stronger than any spell she could ever weave, he gestured at the bare ground.

Tansy, moving with the promised obedience,

finished shucking her own clothing before she dropped and spread herself upon the dirt and leaves. When first she lay with Ossian, she'd expected him to please her. Now she wanted to please this man, however he demanded.

"I dreamed of this while awake," he said hoarsely as he stood surveying her. "But there was firelight."

There would be firelight next time. "We have no need of firelight. There is the moon."

"So there is."

He knelt between her thighs, a proud man coming to her. She could feel stones and twigs digging into her naked back; she could smell the virgin ground, rife with damp. Her breasts peaked in the cool air, and she prayed he would take her soon. Any way he chose.

He laid his palm on her breast and her whole body leaped in response. A growl of demand came from her throat, and he smiled at her.

Oh, and he so seldom smiled. It stole the last of her breath.

"Please," she whispered.

"Are you going to beg, Tansy Bellrose Gant?"

"If I must."

"We canna' have that."

He replaced his palm with his mouth, hot and hungry, and she nearly convulsed with pleasure. Aye, and he seemed to find naught wanting in her diminutive size, for he devoured her, taking her into him, making her flesh his own. She wrapped her legs around him and pulled him closer in.

"Delicious. You taste like heaven." He gasped the words, his breath skittering across her wet flesh. "How can that be, and you a witch?"

Tansy sought for words—clever, barbed ones such as she usually employed—and found none. He gazed into her eyes and her heart stuttered in her chest.

Oh, holy hell, she would no' survive this. She did not want to.

"Let us see how obedient you are, bonny Tansy. Kiss me."

She fused her open mouth to his. She breathed into him and felt him breathe into her also, and gasped as his tongue met hers. Something inside her, always tight and unyielding, melted, and an unnamed pain slid away, replaced with passion so hot it threatened to consume them both.

He murmured, his mouth still fast to hers, a hum deep in his throat, a vibration. Her whole body screamed for him to slide into her.

And then he did, and her mind exploded a split second before her body followed in wave upon wave of exquisite pleasure.

****

"Quick. That was too quick." Malcolm buried his face in Tansy's hair, which smelled of thyme, and held tight. She still trembled in his arms, and he remained inside her. A wonder he could speak at all.

He felt…powerful, vulnerable, victorious, and lost, greedy, and sated. He wanted this moment to last forever, even as he knew it could not.

Ah, God, she fitted him like his own skin. Never had he known such comfort, or imagined it.

"I am sorry."

"Sorry?" She repeated the word as if she'd never before heard it.

"I would ha' lasted longer for you."

"We went up like flame." She laughed softly. "No holding back flame, when it erupts. But, my fine Sir Knight…" She ran her fingers through his sweated hair. "Next time you can tak' as long as you like."

"Will there be a next time, Tansy Bellrose Gant?"

"If you ask; I am ever obedient."

That made him laugh along with her. It also made him grow hard inside her, imagining Tansy Bellrose Gant obedient.

On her knees, perhaps. Och, God!

He kissed her slowly, deeply, seeking each drop of sweetness her mouth contained. They began to move without word or intention, there in the moonlight.

Aye, and it took longer this time, but not enough. Never enough.

Wondrous lass! Splendid, dangerous lass. She had enchanted him.

****

Tansy Bellrose Gant slept. Malcolm wrapped her in a blanket and left her to it while he collected wood and lit a fire beneath the single eye of the moon. They had mated together on the forest floor like beasts of the wild. What had he been thinking? He crouched in front of the fire and slanted a look at her. Immediately, his crotch tightened.

What in hell ailed him? He had not been so far beyond control since the age of sixteen. He'd supposed indulging himself with her would answer the craving and be the cure. Instead, the desire had merely intensified.

He needed to master himself.

Yet look how she slept, curled on her side in unconscious grace, one hand against her cheek. Her lashes showed very black against her pale skin, in the moonlight. Her hair streamed like a river of ebony.

Not the sort of woman who usually caught his eye. He preferred lasses like Catha, fair and rosy.

Catha. How could he have thrust his mission to the back of his mind even for a moment?

Tansy stirred where she lay. She unwound like a wee squirrel in its nest, and her gaze found him beside the fire.

He quickened as if lashed by a whip of desire. Aye, he could not trust himself near this woman. He could not...

"You left me," she accused softly.

"I wished only to keep you warm." He indicated the fire.

"I can think of a better way." She opened the blanket to him; he caught a glimpse of one delicate shoulder. His whole body leaped.

Christ, he could not possibly want her again. Not so soon.

Yet he approached her like a man drawn by chains and stood looking down at her. She smiled—a smile as old as time itself, ancient as the first man and woman, soft and knowing.

"Forget the fire, Sir Knight, and come back to bed."

Chapter Thirteen

And why couldn't Tansy manage to read the expression on Sir Malcolm's face? The newly kindled fire provided enough light, even if it left his eyes dark and unfathomable. She saw desire, aye. Given what they'd shared, he could scarcely deny that.

What they'd shared.

For an instant her mind stuttered over the magnificence of it, the sharp and almost painful perfection. Nothing in coupling with Ossian had prepared her for Malcolm. Even her agile tongue possessed no words.

Yet men were perilous creatures, prone to changing their minds when the fires subsided. Just so had Ossian done. And a hesitance had now come to this man's bearing.

"Get up," he bade her. He said it gently, but she heard iron behind it.

"Nay, but I would prefer…"

He drew a breath and repeated, "Get up, mistress, please, that we may speak together."

"We may speak here." Greatly daring she added, "In one another's arms."

He turned away. Dismay speared Tansy, and she scrambled up hastily.

As if unable to prevent himself, he swiveled his head and watched her. So she made sure to step from the blanket naked, affording him a good look at all he'd just enjoyed.

And aye, he watched that also, and stiffened where he stood.

"Where are my clothes?" she asked archly. "The new ones I brought away from Crag Corvan."

"There. And there and…"

"Never mind. For now, the blanket will serve." She drew it back around her and, barefoot, stepped up to him.

He had only half dressed. He wore his leggings and the tunic open down his chest. It would be the work of but a moment to get him out of those things.

Yet they stood so, unmoving and regarding one another, he towering above her and the firelight dancing over them both.

"What is it you wish to say?"

"Please sit."

"This is well enough." She reached for him, placed her palm against his chest as he'd laid his over her breast earlier. She could feel his heart tripping as if he'd run a great distance.

His face still unreadable, he said, "Mistress Tansy, I maun apologize. I took advantage of you."

"Aye." She stepped still closer. "And might do so again."

He plucked her hand from his chest and held it in his. "Nay, mistress."

Ah—if he thought that having joined with him once—twice—she would be able to exist without him, he must be mad.

"Here," he insisted. "Sit."

He led her down beside the fire, which winked and

smoked in the dark. Did he seek to avoid looking at her? Mayhap, yet he retained her hand in his, and she could feel his heat.

She could smell him, too, and the scent of their coupling, both now burned into her soul.

"List to me, Mistress Tansy. I ha' no wish to harm you."

"You ha' no' harmed me." Ignited her perhaps, touched her deeply, possibly even claimed her. "Is a woman no' made to join wi' a man? What harm can there be, and her willing?"

That made him glance at her. "I might ha' been far more gentle. I lost my head."

"You may come to me sweetly and gently next time."

He stiffened. "There will be no next time."

"Eh?" Tansy's disappointment hit her in the gut, hard. She could say no more.

"I canna' allow the distraction. List to me, mistress. I thank you for your kindness. It was…"

Apparently he had no words for it either; his deep voice died, and they stared at one another, equally helpless.

His fingers contracted on hers painfully. From somewhere she dredged up a protest. "It was more than kindness on my part. You ken that fine. Do you suppose we can travel together wi'out that happening again?"

"Nay."

"Then—"

"Mistress Gant, you promised obedience."

"And I offer it. Do you want me here and now? Anywhere along the trail? On my back, on my knees? Clothed or bare? You have but to snap your fingers, Sir

Knight." By the holy light, what had happened to her pride? That same which had kept her head high through all the past slurs and insults, that allowed her to believe herself above all?

Did she truly mean to surrender it to this man with his strong hands and the fire in his kiss?

He swallowed hard and licked his lips. No man, she told herself, could refuse such an offer—none. And in truth, she fair panted to provide the promised service.

But he said, "Nay. If you would keep your pledge of obedience, you will turn back for Aberdeen come first light. Taking you wi' me is too dangerous."

Tansy's heart dropped violently, and her eyes burned. He did no' want her. She would not weep, she would not! Not for him or any man.

She never wept. Not when the evil Ranna bribed her wee brothers to throw stones at her, not when she heard the whispers about her mother. Certainly not when Ossian turned away from her.

And not now.

She lifted her chin and engaged Malcolm's gaze. "Fool!" she spat. "Do you suppose it easily found, what we just shared?"

"Nay."

"Yet you would toss it away like 'twas naught?"

"You promised to obey. I bid you go."

"And I say—"

"There is no arguing it, mistress. Now dress yousel' and let the discussion be done."

She did not shift from her place. Folding her arms across her breasts stubbornly, she stared into the fire, and the moments slipped by like bats on the wing.

At last she asked, "Is it because I am a witch?" She

never should have suggested as much to him. Better the line she'd taken when he rescued her from the post at the crossroads, that of being wrongly accused.

She'd trusted him too much, a thing that, like weeping, she did very seldom.

He gave an incredulous laugh. "You do admit it, then?"

She shrugged and made no answer. She had as good as admitted it to him before. But her heart thudded, telling her she'd doomed herself on more than one front, trusting him when he did not want her.

Yet he said, "Nay, that is not why. Though 'tis mad for anyone to travel wi' you. We could both be accused, I by association."

"Then why?"

"This task I maun accomplish..."

"Freeing your brother."

"Aye. 'Twill be a hard and perilous road, one that will tax me in all ways."

"I may be of help."

"I think not."

"Aye, but Sir Malcolm, I ha' abilities you can use or that I, at least, could use on your behalf."

He stared at her. "You expect me to condone the use o' witchcraft?"

"'Tis not the dark and terrible thing you suppose, or that people fear. 'Tis part of the natural world, and the power that exists all around us. Rather than spells, it is *knowing*. It is persuasion. In the right circumstances I could, if you need it, give someone a wee push..."

"Did you *push* me to lie wi' you?"

"There was no need. You want me even as I want you. Let us at least be honest wi' it."

He got to his feet, suddenly restless, and took a turn about the fire. Tansy's heart quivered in her breast. Might he reconsider and permit her to accompany him?

But he asked, "How did you come by this ability to push at folk?"

"I did no' come by it. It has always been inside me." *Dhe*, and she exposed more and more of herself to him—too much.

"I ha' heard witches sue the devil for their abilities."

"Nay, 'tis no' like that. At least not for me. Please sit down."

To her surprise he did, though not so close she could easily touch him.

Engaging his eyes, she said, "I do no' ken aught about other women or men who claim the name of witch. I encountered none in Slurt, and can speak only for mysel'. I am no' at all sure I believe in the devil, and what lies inside me has little to do wi' evil, unless I use it in a hurtful way." She considered. "Which I maun admit, I ha' done from time to time, though no' on any grand scale, you ken. Just wee things, to make Ranna trip in a puddle, or…"

He interrupted. "Just what does lie inside you?"

"I am no' certain I can explain. 'Tis an urge like that which comes in the spring when things start to growing. 'Tis a knowing and a force of will A…a twisting o' the will, into persuasion."

He narrowed his dark gaze on her. "It must be powerfully tempting to use."

"Och, it is."

"And mayhap not so innocent as you would ha' it seem. For a man would no' ken when he was being persuaded."

"You still think I swayed you, tricked you into my arms?"

"I am no' at all sure what I think. You say this ability has always been inside you and is no' from the devil? From whence did it come?"

"I do believe it came to me from my mother. I do no' remember her, but folk talk. In Slurt, they talk loudly. She too was branded a witch and ran off when yet I was a bairn, abandoning Father and me. Da married Bessie after that, who raised me." Yet her mother's shadow had never cleared from her—she dwelt within it yet.

Malcolm grunted. "None o' you ever heard from your mother again?"

"Nay. She may be alive or dead—may have got herself burned as a witch. I canna' tell. But Da was no' surprised when my abilities came to light. They must be enough like hers that he recognized them."

"I am sorry you never knew her; 'tis a hard thing. But you maun see you could prove a dangerous companion—one I canna' afford."

"How might I prove dangerous to you? If I keep all I possess—all I am—to myself, only you will know."

"I need to concentrate on the task ahead."

"Tell me of this task o' yours, Sir Malcolm. Sit you quietly and trust me wi' all."

To Malcolm's own surprise, he did.

Chapter Fourteen

"Is that the place? It looks unco' grand." Tansy breathed the words as they peered from the backs of their horses under cover of the trees.

"It is grand," Malcolm told her. "Mistress Catha is a woman of means." He glanced at Tansy with misgiving. Two days on the trail and he almost thought he could sense the thoughts moving in that black head of hers. Even though they had not lain together again, whispers of their connection remained.

He'd resisted taking her once more only by a grand effort of will. That did not keep him from doubting himself or the wisdom of having brought her along with him.

Quite likely the most foolish thing he'd ever done. Though she did have a way of wriggling into his confidence.

Confession, they said, proved good for the soul. But a man needs must be careful to whom he confessed. Tansy and he now carried each other's secrets. It lent them a certain power over one another, with which he did not feel quite comfortable.

Trust did not come easily to him, and trusting an admitted witch seemed the height of foolishness. He risked not only his own safety but Mercien's.

Tansy murmured, "And you wish to abduct the mistress of all that?"

"Whisht! Do no' speak it aloud."

She turned her uncanny eyes on him. "I will no' breathe a word into the wrong ears. Do you tak' me for a fool?"

"Nay." Whatever else Mistress Tansy Bellrose Gant might be, she was clever. "And I do no' *wish* to abduct her. You ken how I am pressed."

"Aye."

"She and I are friends."

Mistress Tansy continued to gaze at him, seeing too much. Did she see how he felt about Catha? That he'd loved her since both of them were children? And now he had to cause her the worst kind of harm.

By heaven, he hated himself.

Tansy quirked an eyebrow but did not demure. "Do you mean to sit here gazing upon the place all day, or will we ride in?"

"Give me but a moment." To consult with his heart and his conscience. To seek, in the rat's nest of his mind, another way he might win Mercien's freedom.

"'Twill not be easy to talk this friend o' yours from the safety o' this place. She will have guards and will be carefully looked after."

"Aye."

"A good thing you brought me. It may come to a matter of persuasion after all."

****

"Malcolm!" The squeal of delight coming from the woman who greeted them in the hall sounded as if it should issue from the throat of a young girl. Indeed, Mistress Catha looked little more than that. Malcolm had explained how she'd been married off and widowed when but a child, but Tansy had not expected her to look quite so youthful still.

Nor so bonny.

Golden hair, a slim, lithesome figure, and skin like rose petals all marked the woman who threw herself into Malcolm's arms. Tansy, forced to stand back and watch while Malcolm wrapped those arms around her, and to observe the expression that came to his face, bit her lip in agony.

They loved each other—that much a blind woman could see. Was it the love of sister for brother? Or more?

Mistress Catha's feet left the floor as Malcolm swept her up. His lips grazed her cheek before he set her down again.

"Och, Malcolm, 'tis grand to see you. I did not know you were yet back from France. I did pray for you, so I do vow, every single day."

The woman's beautiful eyes moved beyond Malcolm and passed over Tansy without really seeing her. "But where is Mercien?"

"That is a story I maun tell." Malcolm's deep voice roughened with his agitation.

Mistress Catha laid her hands against her heart. "Do no' tell me, you ha' come wi' ill news?"

"Very ill indeed."

All the rosy color fled her face. "Never say he…has perished?"

"Nay."

"Nay." She struggled to draw a breath. "For I should know here, inside." For an instant Catha's face lit again, like a beacon.

Malcolm glanced around at the servants thronging the entryway. "Let us go speak somewhere more private. I will tell you all."

Would he? From his guarded expression and the hesitance Tansy felt in him, she doubted it.

"Of course." Catha succeeded in focusing on Tansy. "And who is this?"

"My traveling companion, Mistress Gant."

"Traveling companion?" Catha's brows rose. "Since when ha' you had need of any, besides Mercien?"

"Catha, I will explain all."

"Very well." Mistress Catha turned to Tansy. "Mistress Gant, welcome to Castle Gunn. Maggie, here, will show you to quarters—I am thinking the yellow room, Maggie—and offer you refreshment. You must be eager to rest."

Tansy was eager to hear what Malcolm said to Mistress Catha, but she saw the reflection of the word *obedience* in his eyes. So she bowed her head.

"Thank you kindly, mistress."

"Malcolm, come." Catha linked her arm through Malcolm's and dragged him off through a doorway on the left. He never so much as glanced back at Tansy.

Forgotten? She did not like to think so. Neither did she like how it felt watching him go.

****

"I cannot believe it. Mercien, a prisoner? And your men all lost in France, with not one to keep watch at your back. Oh, sweet Jesu, what's to be done?" Catha pressed her fingers to her mouth and held tight. Malcolm hoped she didn't mean to vomit or swoon.

But the lass, made of stronger stuff than that, soon rallied. "Tell me what I can do to save him. Do you need a ransom? I can provide it. I've more wealth than I can ever spend."

Malcolm hesitated. He had given Catha a much-expunged version of what had befallen him and Mercien, daring not to tell her all. Would a large payment to Latham serve? He thought not; Latham desired Catha along with her fortune.

"My father sent money, all he could spare. I did no' mean to involve you in this, Catha. I but wished to give you the ill tidings. I ken fine what Mercien means to you."

"Do you?" She got to her feet and turned her back to him. "I do no' think so."

"We are like family," he asserted carefully.

That made her turn back to him with a sad smile. "You, Malcolm, are like family to me. A dear brother. We ha' known each other from time out o' mind. For Mercien"—she drew a breath—"my feelings are far different."

And Malcolm found that hurt after all. He loved his brother. More than himself? Unquestionably. Why, then, did it pain him to see Catha gift Mercien with her heart? "Why did you never tell him?" he asked softly.

"How could I? Bundled off into that marriage almost before I realized the truth of my feelings for him. And after…"

"You have been a free woman for two years. You might have said."

"And him awa' most that time, in France. I wanted to make certain I was the woman he deserved—here, inside myself." She clasped her hands to her breast. "That marriage, Malcolm—it changed me. Mayhap even ruined me."

Malcolm studied her frankly. "How?" She could

not look more perfect. "You are strengthened, perhaps—tempered as in a fire."

"Aye, and before that, broken. Because, dearest Malcolm, there is strength of spirit and strength of flesh. Sometimes they are one and the same; sometimes no'."

Malcolm thought of the dark hours chained in Latham's vile cell. Aye, and anger had kept his spirit strong—anger and hate. What of Mercien? What buoyed him up?

He nodded reluctantly.

She came and sat across from him. "I shall tell you a secret, Malcolm. You recall I said things did not go easily for me in my husband's home."

"Aye."

"Aye," she echoed softly. "I had barely fifteen years when I went to him. And I lost bairn after bairn." Sorrow filled her eyes. "Once I gained my freedom at his death, I consulted wi' the best physicians. 'Tis their considered opinion I will ne'er bear a living child." Her gaze fell abruptly. "I could no' ask that of Mercien, to live wi'out issue. I ken fine what it means to a man, having a son."

"But..." Would Mercien care? Aye so, he would care, any man would. But Malcolm doubted it would keep him from a life at Catha's side.

Still, deep sadness touched him. "I am that sorry for what you suffered at the hands o' your husband."

Her eyes grew brilliant with tears. "Do you ken how I remember Mercien? How I did, all that time I remained in my husband's hands? Laughing, always laughing, his eyes alight. And that smile—I could ne'er help but smile when I saw it. Always teasing and spinning silly flights o' fancy. He was my strength, then. But such a man should ha' bairns. He should infect them wi' his laughter and tuck them into their wee beds at night."

Abruptly, she broke. Malcolm did not know if she cried for old wounds or new, but his heart ached in his chest. Aye so, Mercien had always carried light within him. Malcolm could not but wonder whether, by now, it would have winked out, shut away in pain and darkness.

"Whisht, lass." He drew Catha into his arms. And how many times had he longed to have her there? Now his heart broke all over again. For he must hurt her far more than she'd already been hurt, if he meant to save Mercien, betray her in the worst possible manner.

How could he betray a woman who trusted him? Aye, and how could he leave his brother languishing in the blackness of Latham's cell?

Chapter Fifteen

The scratch at Malcolm's door interrupted his endless pacing and momentarily distracted him from the dark thoughts in his mind.

Who might it be at this late hour? For the household slept, even Catha gone to her chamber. Dinner, hours ago, had been grim and nearly silent, Catha pale from hearing his news, and he half strangled with his grief.

Only Tansy had partaken heartily of the fine fare, speaking little and watching them both with her all-seeing eyes.

He swung wide the door now to reveal her standing, just as if his thoughts had conjured her. She wore naught but a white chemise, her tiny feet once more bare, and her black hair hung loose around her, swirling slightly in the eddies of air. The flame of the candle she carried bent and swayed also, as if bowing to him.

"What are you doing here?" he whispered. "You should be fast asleep."

"I could not sleep, not in my own bed. Will I come in?"

Not in her own bed. What was that supposed to mean? Did she think to take her rest in his? Even as his body responded to the idea, he blocked her way. "Nay."

"But we need to speak."

Speak, was it? "We can do so in the morning."

"Now. My room is three doors down fro' yours, but still I could feel that you were awake. It may help, getting things off your mind."

It might help to kiss her, stoke the fire he knew lay inside her. To drag her to the bed and plunge inside her over and over again. Suddenly it seemed the best idea he'd had since he left France.

She sidled past him, her body brushing against his; just like that, he came alight. He swore bitterly, and she set the candle down before turning to face him.

"Out wi' it. Tell me what is keeping you fro' your rest."

He replied to the request with a question. "You say you could feel me awake?"

"Aye. It seems some sort o' connection has formed between us."

Malcolm scowled, not certain he liked that. Before he could decide, she went and perched on his bed, which had seen little enough of his presence this night. She said, "I thought, Sir Malcolm, I might provide you some comfort."

His throat closed. "Comfort?"

"Aye, a friendly ear—or anything else you need. Tell me what torments you so."

"You know very well. 'Tis Catha. You ha' seen her, listened to her. You must be able to tell what she is—warm, honest, and loving. She trusts me. How can I betray her? And yet if I'm to save Mercien, what other choice ha' I?"

"You love her." Tansy said it softly but with certainty.

"Of course I love her. What man would no'? Every

part of me cries out to protect her. Instead I maun deliver her to that villain. Impossible! She has already endured one hellish marriage. And aye, Latham will wed wi' her. He wants her wealth and her property."

"And what of Mistress Catha? Does she return your love?"

"Like a brother, she says." He grimaced.

"Does she love Mercien?"

"Och, aye. That does not mak' it right for me to sacrifice her for his sake. Will Mercien ever forgive me if I do?" Would his father forgive him if he did not?

"It sounds to me as if this villain, Latham, desperately needs to die."

That captured all Malcolm's attention. "Aye so, but how? He lurks like a beast in that stronghold o' his, all his men about him."

"Too bad you do not ha' the acquaintance o' a witch who might be willing to act on your behalf."

He stepped closer to the bed. "Is that possible? Could a witch do aught to help?"

"I do no' ken, do I? But such a woman, loyal to you," she paused significantly, "bonded wi' you, might be able to help accomplish the deed."

"B-bonded wi' me?" he stuttered, able to do nothing but repeat the words.

She smiled the same smile she'd given him back in the wood and said, "My braw Sir Knight, come to bed."

****

Tansy watched through slitted eyes while Malcolm stripped off his tunic, the blood thrumming in her veins. His dark gaze never left her as he tossed the garment on the floor and reached to unfasten his leggings. She wished she could understand the craving for him that rode her, continuous and relentless, a bright need demanding to be assuaged.

A right eyeful he made and no mistake, when the leggings joined the tunic on the floor. Apart from his wounds, he could not be more pleasing as he stood before her, his black hair loose, the candlelight caressing the muscles of shoulders, chest, and thighs.

And below…aye well, she knew fine he made an even better handful than an eyeful.

"Come here," she bade again.

One eyebrow quirked. He did not move even though he already stood proud for her. "Who is it giving the orders?"

"It is I."

"Even though 'twas you swore to obedience?"

"Come here, Sir Knight. 'Twill be to your advantage."

He took two steps but said, "This will solve nothing."

"Will it no'?" She sat up and drew her gown over her head, marking how his eyes lit when her bare skin came into view. "'Twill bring you comfort and further strengthen our bonds."

"Do I want our bonds strengthened?"

"If you wish for my help."

"Would you so compel me to couple wi' you?"

A good question, but Tansy did not hesitate with her reply. "I have a powerful hunger for the taste o' you. I will do as I must."

That drew him the rest of the way to the bed. As soon as he came within reach, she reached out and caressed him, before wrapping her fingers tight. "Ah, Sir Malcolm, but you are beautiful."

"As are you, wee witch."

"Do you think so?" She near preened with delight.

"Och, aye." He came down onto the bed. The candle flickered and went out. "Ah," he murmured in her ear, "we maun light that again."

"Why?" She sounded breathless.

"I want to see the look in your eyes when I am inside you."

"Aye, but first I've this terrible craving to ease." She leaned forward, open mouthed, to taste his skin. Throat, chest, stomach. By mere touch, she followed the tantalizing path made by the line of black hair that bisected the rippled muscles of his abdomen, moving ever downward. She still had her fingers wrapped around him when she bent further to taste him, a delicate flick of her tongue.

He gasped and stiffened in every limb. "Tansy."

Her name on his lips tumbled her over the edge. Hair falling forward, she bent and enfolded him with her lips, caressed him with lavish care before she paused and asked, "Have you never done this before?"

"Nay." He sounded hoarse. "We heard about it in France but never—"

"Nor ha' I, but it seems natural wi' you."

"Surely such pleasure maun be a sin."

"Aye, surely it must. Do you care?" Not awaiting a reply, she took him into her mouth again. The persuasions of her tongue soon had him moving, flexing those wonderful muscles, as hard as iron inside her mouth.

Lithesome, she bowed her body and released her hold on him, but only so she might wrap her hands around his buttocks instead and draw him deeper in.

Malcolm groaned and buried his hands in her hair, fingers cradling her skull. "Tansy. Tansy, I will surely lose my senses."

The intensity of her pleasure made it impossible to reply. If he thought she'd release him now for mere words…

"Easy, lass." His grip on her hair became pressure. "We canna'—"

She could. She wanted all of him, heat and taste. Her magnificent, beautiful knight.

She made a sound in her throat, one of utter surrender. His control broke at almost the same instant and, hot and sudden, he yielded to her what she desired.

The shock and delight of it went through her, a stab of pure bliss. Completeness beyond describing. A wealth of feeling scalded her, so powerful that for an instant the world and all it contained fell away.

"Tansy." He caressed her hair, her cheeks, and drew her into his arms. The tenderness of it undid her still further and made it impossible to speak.

A good man, Sir Malcolm Montgomery. One with kindness in him. One to whom she might present her heart.

But nay, for love brought only vulnerability, and vulnerability pain. She could not—

Before she might complete the thought, he released her. Protest arose; she whimpered and clung to him. "Nay."

"Whisht, lass. I go only to strike the light." Freeing himself from her, he did as much; the weak flame gained strength and allowed her to see him standing beside the bed, tall and strong.

His gaze caressed her slowly—lips, breasts, and

thighs—before he said, "I hope you do no' suppose we are done. Tansy Bellrose Gant, I mak' good on my promises."

"Aye," she whispered, "and the night is long."

Chapter Sixteen

"A word, mistress, if you do no' mind."

Catha looked round at Tansy, who hovered in the doorway of the dining hall, where breakfast had been laid. Dim morning light flooded through the narrow windows, and rain fell outside.

Tansy had left Sir Malcolm sleeping, resisting with difficulty the desire to touch him again. His exhaustion—and the lurid wounds that still marked him—argued he needed his rest.

Besides, she wished to speak with Catha alone.

Catha made a gesture of invitation. "To be sure. Come in, please, and break your fast. I trust you spent a pleasant night."

Tansy strove to hide her smile and failed. "I did, mistress." She peered into the room, which seemed overfilled with servants. "But I did hope we might speak alone."

"Aye, so?" Catha lifted elegantly curved brows. "Let us then repair to my wee parlor. Come."

The parlor, a small chamber at the back of the house, the room where Mistress Catha clearly pursued her sewing, lay dim and very nearly cold, a poor fire smoldering in the grate.

Catha stirred it to life and indicated one of the benches. "Pray sit and say what you will. I maun admit, Mistress Gant, I am curious about you. Never before ha' I known Malcolm to associate wi' any woman, much less travel wi' one. May I ask how you met?"

"That is a story in itself. Perhaps you will allow me to share it at another time."

"As you wish." Catha studied Tansy closely. "What is it troubles you?"

Tansy hesitated. She'd contemplated this step long, lying in Malcolm's arms while he slept, but still did not know for sure whether she acted as she should. Malcolm would not be happy with her.

Yet she'd sworn to aid him in any way possible.

She returned Catha's gaze and asked, "Might I speak honestly? I ken fine we ha' just met."

"Please do speak honestly." Catha perched on the bench across from her. "I strive my best to be an earnest woman and deal honestly wi' everyone, having learned the damage lies can do."

Tansy nodded. She, on the other hand, had built her life on half-truths. But that was before Malcolm.

"'Tis about Sir Malcolm and his brother—their predicament."

Catha's attention quickened. "Has Malcolm told me all?"

"Nay, I do no' believe so."

"Aye, and I thought not. I can always tell when he is withholding something. But you will tell me?"

Tansy drew a breath. If she did, would Malcolm ever forgive her?

She answered the question with another. "What do you know o' this Latham who holds Sir Malcolm's brother a prisoner?"

"Enough. He is held in high esteem by the King, one of his right-hand men. He is also ruthless, with a reputation for cruelty."

"You have met him?"

"Many times. My father knew his family from the time I was a wee child. More lately, my husband often went to court and took me wi' him. Donald Latham was frequently there."

"He must, then, be a man of means."

"Unquestionably."

"One who often gets what he wants."

"Mistress Gant, if you ha' a point to this, I pray you speak out."

Tansy leaned closer on her bench. "Sir Malcolm has told you this villain, Latham, fell upon him and his brother when they landed from France. He's said they were taken prisoner and held several weeks."

"Aye."

"Did he also tell you they were tortured?"

Mistress Catha's lovely face closed. "Nay, he did no'."

"This vile excuse for a man wished to persuade Sir Malcolm to do his will. Sir Malcolm's wounds are many and livid."

"You have seen?" Mistress Catha's gaze questioned her.

"I have. Yet, as Sir Malcolm confessed to me, Latham reserved the worst of his cruelty for Sir Mercien, knowing that would hurt Sir Malcolm worse than his own pain."

Mistress Catha's hands gripped one another so tightly the fingers turned white. "So it would. I ha' known them both since we were all wee bairns. Malcolm always made it his place to look after Mercien, even after Mercien, a knight in his own right, no longer needed such care." She sucked in a breath. "And Mercien remains in Latham's hands."

"Aye."

"Then we maun free him—at any cost."

"Any cost, mistress?"

"Aye, I ha' told Malcolm I will aid him in launching an attack against Latham, if he will. Lend him members of my household guard, since he is wi'out his own men."

"That will no' serve." Tansy hesitated and, swiftly, consulted the knowledge—and daring—within. "Sir Malcolm may throw himself against the stones of that keep until he breaks." Or until he died—indeed, 'twas just that Tansy feared. "Do you think Latham would have undertaken this scheme if he did not believe he could keep hold of his prisoner? Nay, mistress, Sir Mercien will be released only in exchange for another."

Mistress Catha reared back. "And who is that?"

"You."

****

Malcolm woke slowly to the pain of his wounds, as he had now for days uncounted. Possession of his mind—which surely had come close to breaking in Latham's dungeon—returned to him more slowly still, in pieces, as it were.

He lay in a soft bed that smelled clean, and daylight, dim and gray, pressed against his eyelids, so night must be past. Yet his deep exhaustion, barely touched, remained with him as well as…

Another hunger, barely assuaged—for the touch, the taste of the wee witch lass. White, agile limbs, a still more agile tongue, black hair wrapped around them both, and the raw, intoxicating taste of her. Pleasure so sharp even the memory of it made his heart leap.

His eyes flew open. The chamber lay empty except for Malcolm himself, naked as she had left him. Someone must have come in while he slept and lit the fire. Had Tansy gone before that, in an effort to maintain the propriety of the household?

It did not seem like something she would do. His wee witch did not concern herself overmuch with propriety.

Sprawled on his back in the bed, he contemplated the things she had done with him—and to him—last night. Turned him inside out right proper she had, stolen a piece of him. Given a piece back too, quite possibly. He grew hard just thinking on it.

He needed to find her, gaze into those pale, uncanny eyes of hers—the same ones that glowed with magical light when he entered her—and...well, ground himself, he supposed. He had no words for the way he felt toward Tansy Bellrose Gant. Just emotions, and he'd never been good at naming those.

Perhaps, when it came to this woman, names did not matter.

He climbed from the bed and dressed hastily, not waiting to confine his hair in its thong of leather, so it hung loose on his shoulders. Servants he encountered outside the dining hall directed him to Catha's private chamber. He tapped on the door and walked in to hear her say, "Me?"

Both women froze with their heads close together, leaning from opposite benches, before they looked at him guiltily. At least, Catha appeared startled and guilty; the expression in Tansy's eyes held something more. Chagrin? Regret?

His heart clenched in his chest. "What are you doing here?"

Tansy sprang to her feet. Her hands—the same that had been all over him during the night—tangled together.

"I ha' told Mistress Catha the truth."

"What?" It came from him in a roar. His men and his horses alike might attest he rarely raised his voice, save in battle. Now the agonized word burst from him.

"She has a right to know. She loves him, Sir Malcolm. And 'tis her safety at stake."

Catha rose also and spun to face Malcolm. His spirit recoiled at the look in her eyes. "Did you truly mean to betray me, Malcolm? After all we ha' been to each other? Like family, just."

"If I had to." Right after he finished strangling the wee witch. Or handing her over to the Royal Commission, which might be preferable.

Catha looked as if he had slapped her. He stepped farther into the room and shut the door, measuring Catha as he did so. It would be easier to take her by force out on the road than here beneath the noses of her household guard. But Tansy might just have spoiled his chances of persuading her away.

Catha's cheeks flamed. "So 'tis me Latham wants."

"Aye."

"As a price for Mercien."

"Aye, Catha."

She stared at him long while none of them so much as breathed. Then something in her stance eased. "'Tis a fair trade."

"Eh?" he gaped at her and, angry as he felt, shot an incredulous look at Tansy.

Catha lifted her chin a notch. "I agree to the exchange."

Malcolm shook his head as if trying to clear his ears. "What did you say?"

"I agree to the exchange—myself for Mercien. I would give far more to win him free."

"Catha—" he began.

She interrupted him. "What did you think o' me, Malcolm, to suppose I would no' care more for him than mysel'? How did you mean to accomplish it? By trickery? By trussing me up like a prize hen and handing me over against my will?"

His throat closed. "Aye." He struggled for breath. "I meant to persuade you to tak' the trail wi' us by telling you Latham—holding you in some regard— might listen to your arguments and release Mercien. Then I intended to give you over to him by force if need be."

"What o' my guard? Did you no' suppose I would take a number of men wi' me?"

"I hoped to convince you a small party travels quickest. And I intended to murder your men if I had to."

Her brows twitched. "Honest, at least."

"I am an honest man. When I can be. I do no' like resorting to deception, Catha, especially where you are concerned."

"And now, thanks to Mistress Tansy, you will no' have to. We will leave directly. Only let me give instructions for the household before I go."

"Catha…"

"I do not ken when—if—I will return."

"Catha, he intends marriage."

Her blue eyes met his, full on. "I ken. 'Tis naught I ha' not endured before."

"But Latham…"

"Is a vile beast who takes pleasure in causing pain to others, aye. But we are speaking of *Mercien. His* pain. His release. I love him, Malcolm. Do you no' ken that? I would give mysel' over a thousand times for his sake."

The truth of that stopped all words in Malcolm's throat.

"And," Catha concluded, "I would ha' wound up in Latham's hands either way, no? For you would ha' handed me over. The only difference is, Mistress Tansy warned me."

"Aye." He bent another look on Tansy, one rife with fury. How could he ever trust her again?

Tansy stiffened in response to his glare but leaned forward and said, "Mistress Catha, your sacrifice will be a brief one. For I ha' determined that this beast, Latham, must die."

Chapter Seventeen

"How did you know?" Malcolm leaned from his saddle close to Tansy's ear and spoke the question.

The day had grown old. Catha, refusing to delay for fear of what torment Mercien might suffer through another night, had insisted on leaving that very noon. They now traveled in a small troop that included the three most trusted members of her guard.

Dun Ballan lay a day and a half's journey on. They would arrive tomorrow night; Malcolm should be thinking of means and strategies. Instead, he seemed able to focus on little but the wee lass with the wild black hair, who rode beside him.

He still ached to throttle her—almost as much as he ached to couple with her again. His body, despite its wounds and weariness, despite his anger, craved her. Oh aye, he wanted to murder her, but he longed to enjoy her first.

She lifted her brows at him. "Eh?"

"Catha. That she'd be willing to sacrifice herself for Mercien, if she heard the truth."

Tansy inspected him slowly, taking her time with it. "I am a woman. I understand what desire might do."

"Desire? Or love?"

"Both. You heard her; she loves him. More than hersel'."

"As do I." More than his conscience.

"Master Mercien is a fortunate man. Not at the present moment, I allow, but in his friends. I canna' help but wonder how 'twould be, to be held in such regard."

"Mistress—"

"Now I ha' won your anger, which is no' what I wished. But my own choices were few: let you pursue your crack-brained scheme…"

"Crack-brained?"

"Did you truly suppose Latham would let you— and Mercien—ride awa' out o' there, prey to your consciences, knowing you might tell what he'd done?"

"Mayhap." Mayhap not. "It would no' matter then what we said. They would ha' been wed."

"And you likely dead." Her uncanny gaze seared him. "You maun see, I could no' let that happen."

"I see 'twas no' up to you. I trusted you to keep my confidence. Instead, you rose straight from my bed and—"

"Aye, so I did. If you canna' see why—"

Catha's mare came nosing in between them. "Bairns, bairns, you grow overloud. If you wish to present your quarrel to the ears of my guard…"

"We do no' quarrel!" Malcolm declared furiously. "I do but reprimand her for—"

"You ha' no right to reprimand me. I am no' your servant nor your wife. If I went to your bed, it was voluntarily. And you may be sure it will no' happen again."

"So it will no'."

"My loves, we maun think o' Mercien. Malcolm, whatever scheme you hatched in your head is no longer viable. We need a new one."

"One that includes Latham's death," Tansy put in.

"Aye. If I wed and then kill him…"

"You will appear before the King, who will then pronounce upon you a sentence o' death."

"Aye," Catha said softly. "But even then, Mercien would be free."

"And heartbroken." Malcolm thought on it. If these lasses opted for honesty, so should he. "Do you think he will wish to live wi'out you, Catha, any more than you wi'out him?"

Catha lit as with inner flame. "We maun, I think, prove devious—more so than Latham himsel'."

"A lofty ambition."

"Aye, but I ha' Mistress Tansy on my side. Do I no', Mistress Tansy?"

"You do."

"So she and I will put our heads together and come up wi' a plan. You, Malcolm, will keep right out o' it."

"What?"

"I agree," Tansy said quickly.

Malcolm drew a breath. "Now, wait just a—"

Catha spoke to Tansy and not him. "We are clever enough, are we not, to best Latham at his own scheming?"

"So we are." Now Tansy leaned in to Catha. "I ha' a secret to tell you, one that may just serve."

"Nay," Malcolm cried.

Both women eyed him. With a jerk of her head, Tansy told Catha, "He knows the secret already. 'Tis tied to how we met."

"I would love to hear how you met."

"So you shall. Just as soon as we pause for the night. Then you and I will make our plans."

I am in deep trouble, Malcolm thought, his heart sinking, for they have joined up against me.

****

Malcolm took another gulp of thin, sour ale and eyed the women at the table opposite his, wondering how his life had slipped so far out of his control. The inn—a poor one, but dimly lit and with abominable accommodations—lay less than a day's ride from Dun Ballan. Tomorrow would see launched the scheme the two women hatched together.

Without him, if they could manage it.

Who would have thought the two of them, so different, would fall into easy confidence, even ready friendship? But so they had. Ignoring their poor dinner, they sat, the light head and the dark nearly touching, speaking ferociously.

Now the hour grew late. Malcolm, abandoned by Catha's guards, who had all gone to bed, brooded alone, unable to take his gaze from the two women.

Quite plainly, the blame for all of this lay at his feet. He never should have rescued Tansy, back at Slurt. Then she could not have enchanted him—thinking on it, he felt sure she had, after all—and she would no' have been able to influence Catha and awaken in her this terrible defiance.

Aye so, he'd known Catha for a strong woman, but this far outdistanced his expectations.

He scowled at Tansy's back—the most he could see of her—and fought his frustration. Had he not rescued her from that post, she'd likely be under questioning by now. He'd never have touched her. Kissed her. Tasted and plunged into her, felt her wild heat. He'd have that lack in his life.

He'd also have his wits and full sanity.

If she hadn't enchanted him there at the crossroads, she'd surely done so the first time they coupled together for, do his damnedest, he could not stop thinking on it, no matter how angered with her he became.

And he had become flamingly angered.

He longed to step up to their table, interrupt their cozy conversation, and declare 'twas he whom his father had sent to free Mercien. But even in his head that sounded too much like the whining of a seven-year-old.

He could not recall the last time he'd whined. Mercien would laugh at him for it—were Mercien still able to laugh.

He slammed his tankard on the scarred table and got up at last. The room, deserted but for the three of them, lay so quiet the women could not miss his movements. Tansy's shoulder twitched, but she did not look round.

He stomped to their table and stood until they both raised their eyes to him. Unsettling, for their eyes, though nothing alike, held similar expressions, cool and calculating.

Catha gave him her sweet smile. "Going to your bed? We mean to retire soon also." The two women were to share a chamber—Malcolm had one of his own.

"I will no' leave you down here by yoursel's."

"Why? The place is empty."

"Will you no' allow me into your discussion," he asked wryly, "seeing as how this venture lies under my dominion?"

They exchanged maddening looks. Catha got to her feet. "You are right; 'tis over late. We will discuss it in the morning, Malcolm."

Frustration crawled up his chest and closed his throat. He cast a hard look at Tansy before whirling on his heel, snatching up a candle, and climbing the narrow steps that led to his assigned chamber, while whispering curses.

He'd no sooner stripped himself down and slipped into the lumpy and malodorous bed than the door of his chamber opened. Tansy sailed in.

He sat up with alacrity. "I hope you ha' come to share wi' me the plans you and Catha made."

"Something like that." She sounded breathless. "I *have* come to share."

"Let me strike a light."

"You and your lights. I need none. I know you now by touch."

Malcolm's body sprang to immediate attention. "Eh? Tansy, we canna'. Not wi' Catha in the house."

"Catha is in her own chamber, and I am in yours. Ha' you any objection?"

He had thousands, starting with the fact that she and Catha refused to confide in him, and including the fact that he, not they, had been entrusted with Mercien's rescue. Not to mention Tansy's failure to keep her vow of obedience. But he did not seem able to speak.

He heard her approach the bed, though he could barely see her in the dim light filtering through the narrow window. Cursed if he did not want to see her, though, as her garments peeled away one by one. Her slender, lithesome body, those pert high breasts seemingly made to fill his mouth, the graceful legs that had a tendency to anchor him to her.

The vile mattress tilted as she planted one knee on it. "Do you, my fine knight, mean to send me awa'?"

"Aye." He spoke it like a man pushing a boulder up a hill. "This is no' wise."

"Wise?" She gave a hiccough of a laugh. "What is wisdom when we may no' be alive tomorrow? When I may ne'er have this chance again?"

Never again to hold her, taste her, ignite her heat—suddenly his whole being desired it. She did not lie. They went to Dun Ballan tomorrow. That did not mean they would ever ride away from there.

She gave him no opportunity to ponder it further. Planting her palm in the center of his chest, she pushed him down where he sat and climbed on top of him. Her legs fastened tight around his hips and pertinent parts of their bodies came together, a screaming agony of pleasure.

"Tansy—"

"Speak my name again. I love how you speak my name." She whispered the request against his lips.

"Tan—"

As soon as he opened his mouth she plunged her tongue inside. His resistance melted in the heat of it like frost before the sun.

Oh, holy sweet Jesu. She would kill him with her passion. A fine end.

She stretched her body atop his in a luxuriant move, skin on skin, breasts abrading the hair on his chest, arms sliding up around his neck, and deepened the kiss. If she went any deeper, she would claim his heart.

He twisted his hands in the wealth of her hair and held on. She began to move slowly, cleaving her body to his, tormenting but not quite granting admittance.

He groaned in protest and she broke the kiss. "Want me, Sir Knight. I want you to want me."

"I want you. Shall I show you?"

"Show me."

He flipped her on her back in one strong move. She may have assumed control of Mercien's rescue, but he was in charge here, tonight.

"Tell me what you want." Now he trickled the words into her ear and felt her shiver as with fever.

"You. This."

"How?"

"I want you inside me. Need you ask?"

"Inside you—where?" He wanted to plunge into her so much he could scarcely breathe; he wanted her to acknowledge him, more.

"Anywhere. Everywhere."

"That," he assured her, "I can surely do."

Chapter Eighteen

"Malcolm is going to be furious." Catha whispered the words even though she and Tansy stood outside the door of the inn and presumably Malcolm, still up in his chamber, would not hear. The two women waited anxiously while Lionel, head of Catha's guard, brought their horses.

"Are you certain he still sleeps?"

"Aye." Tansy wrapped the shawl more closely around her shoulders. "He is spent." Also, she'd given him just a wee push to assure he might stay asleep a bit longer. Then she'd kissed his lips and slipped away, wondering if she would ever see him again.

"He will wake soon. And he will come after us."

"That is why we maun get awa' out o' here at once. Where are those horses?"

Ah, Tansy could see Lionel coming with them now. Her empty stomach—for they had not tarried for breakfast—did a slow roll.

Catha went on fretting. "Have you ever seen him ride when he is angry? I have. No one could best him in a race—not even Mercien."

Catha's voice broke on the last word, and Tansy shot her a look. She wondered if Catha had ever lain with her love.

Tansy's body still tingled from her night with Malcolm, while every single moment remained emblazoned on her mind—every touch, each kiss, each caress.

Not that she loved Sir Malcolm. Did she?

The question caused her eyes to grow wide, but she had no time for contemplating mad things. Lionel arrived with the horses, and the other two guardsmen—Reginald and Burt—stepped forward to help her and Catha mount.

From the mare's back she looked up at the inn and located the window of the chamber where Malcolm slept. It remained dark. Had she used too much magic, or just enough?

She could not fairly say whether she loved the man, but she wanted full well to protect him from falling back into Latham's hands.

"Swiftly," she called, "let us ride."

****

Malcolm woke slowly from a lurid dream, his whole body alive with desire, and lay with his eyes closed for a moment, savoring the sensations. The memories, he corrected himself. For aye, it had all happened. Every tantalizing movement of Tansy's lips.

Tansy.

His mind cried out for her even as his body echoed the demand. She'd come to his bed, hot and eager. They'd fused together in all the ways a man and woman might. He could still taste her, could virtually feel her beside him, feel himself inside her.

Sweet, wild, and beautiful lass with the willing body and clever mind. One in ten thousand.

He opened his eyes to find the chamber filled with dim gray light. The bed beside him lay empty and cold.

Aye then, she would have gone back to Catha's

chamber. Indecent to find her here, and the two of them not wed.

His spirits sank as the memory of what this day must bring descended on him. Catha. Dun Ballan. Mercien.

How could he entertain even a shred of desire? By all that was holy, he had to endanger one of those he loved best in all the world, to try and save the other. And Tansy…

He could not say, in truth, how he felt about her. But the prospect of being in her company drew him from the bed and had him donning his clothing and weapons hastily. She awaited him below. Why did he tarry here?

But she did not await him below.

His arrival in the main room of the inn brought forth a sleepy landlord, who told him the rest of his party had ridden on.

"What is that you say?" Malcolm felt the blood drain from his head. "When?"

"Och, it maun ha' been near an hour ago, Sir Knight."

An hour. Precious time slipping away like sand while he slumbered, dreaming of the lithesome lass with the gleaming eyes. She who had just betrayed him.

Had she planned it all? Had she exhausted him and sent him deep into sleep so she and the others might then depart? What of her promised loyalty? He spoke a curse that made the landlord back off a step.

"My horse. At once."

"Aye, m'lord. Lad—fetch Master's horse at once." The landlord turned to Malcolm, concern now etching his face. "Some ale, m'lord, before you go?"

"Sod that," Malcolm said rudely and went to await his mount.

****

"So that is Dun Ballan." For the first time in hours Tansy found herself distracted from thoughts of Malcolm. Indeed, all the day long she'd focused more of her attention back than forward, half expecting to see an angry Malcolm appear on their trail. They'd ridden hard, yet she knew he'd ride harder, spurred by rage.

To be sure, she'd cast a few wee spells in their wake, meant to delay him—naught that would harm him or his mount, that fine beast, but a few downed tree limbs, a confusing twist in the road, and a broken-down cart in his way could not hurt.

Still, she reckoned they had not much time. They should hasten on and insert themselves into Latham's household. Yet the sight of the keep, a great pile of black stones beneath a brooding gray sky, gave her pause.

"It looks an evil place," she said to Catha.

"It is an evil place, if it holds Mercien in chains." Catha's expression turned uncommonly grim. "And if 'tis anything like its master."

"Have you been here before, Mistress Catha?"

"I have once or twice, by invitation and in my father's company. I believe Latham wished to impress us. All such invitations ceased when my father sold me into marriage."

"Latham wanted you even then? But you were no more than a wee girl."

"He wanted my father's lands. Father chose to send me to another. So you see, things might ha' been still worse than what I endured. All, Mistress Tansy, is

129

known by degrees. Latham is a cruel man with a devious mind. Ruthless. Never turn your back on him. And do no' let him ken you love Malcolm."

"I—"

"Do no' spend your breath trying to deny it. I saw your expression when you came from his chamber this dawn. Latham hates him and will hurt you for that reason—as we ha' learned. Hold your secret close to your breast, even as I will hold mine."

Tansy nodded.

"Then, mistress, if you are ready, let us move on."

Tansy cast one more look over her shoulder before nudging her mare forward with her knees.

The keep loomed over them as they approached. Situated offshore on a scrap of island in a loch, it might be reached only via a wooden bridge guarded by a black tower, from which men immediately emerged. Lionel pushed forward to meet them.

"Good day," he called.

Perhaps not an auspicious beginning, Tansy thought. The day, which had never been fine, had now nearly passed. Dark settled in from the surrounding hills.

Latham's guards raked her and Catha with their gazes and glared at Catha's men. Tansy's inner sense sat up and began to howl. Nay, perhaps this had not been a good idea.

"State your business," said the man on the right, not bothering to lower his sword. Looking up at the tower, Tansy saw the head of an arrow piercing the narrow slit between the stones. "Dun Ballan is closed."

Aye, and looked it.

Lionel, appearing perturbed, persisted. "I ha' here

the Lady Catha of Castle Gunn come to call upon Donald Latham. Kindly tell your master she has come."

"Be off wi' you," said the man callously. "After nightfall, no one comes or goes."

Tansy's heart fell. If they were forced to wait for morning, Malcolm would catch them up. And then how would she be able to protect him?

Catha nudged her horse forward. "Kindly tell Master Latham I am here, unless you wish to lose the skin of your back."

The two men exchanged glances. One of them held up a hand, signaling the tower, before pelting away with his armor rattling.

Tansy, unable to prevent herself, turned in the saddle and looked back the way they'd come. In the moments they'd wasted suing for entry, night had indeed fallen. She doubted she would be able to see Malcolm now, in any case.

He might be just there, watching them. His anger might bring him forward, and the guard in the tower might well release his shot. Malcolm might fall.

Despair assailed her at the thought. For an instant she could not breathe.

Then Catha, returned to her side, nudged her. "Best say a prayer; that man returns."

So swiftly? Tansy spun about to see the guard, well winded, jogging toward them.

"Let them pass," he called to his fellows. "At once!"

Relief and terror combined to drench Tansy with hot and cold. She did not want to enter this place. Some deep and primordial instinct within told her to flee even as her heart rejoiced: Malcolm at least would not be able to follow them in.

Catha, head high, moved forward. Lionel followed, only to be halted by the breathless guard.

"Nay—only the women."

"Eh?" Lionel balked, hand on his sword. "Unacceptable. I am Mistress MacGunn's escort. Where she goes, so go I."

"Only the women, or I am to turn you all awa'."

Catha raised her gaze to the pile of black stones of which Dun Ballan had been built. Mercien lay there: Tansy could almost hear her thinking the words. So close to him, how could she leave?

"Mistress." Lionel engaged her attention. "I beg you at least wait for morning."

"Another night?" Catha whispered. More torment for Mercien. She turned to Tansy. "I will go. You do no' need to come wi' me."

"But we ha' a plan," Tansy protested in a whisper, far weaker than she liked.

"Aye, but you need no' risk your safety."

How could she let Catha face this terrible place alone? Without Tansy's particular abilities, she might never emerge again.

Once more she glanced behind and whispered not a prayer but a wee spell.

"Keep him safe."

And then she rode forward at Catha's side, into the darkness.

Chapter Nineteen

"What do you mean they ha' gone ahead wi'out me? Wi'out you?" Frustration once more clawed at Malcolm's throat, nearly choking him. He'd reached the accursed end of his journey following delay after delay, only to find the members of Catha's household guard riding back to meet him. "And you let them?"

"I did try and persuade Mistress MacGunn to wait. My lady insisted. What was I to do, Sir Malcolm?"

"What were you to do? Overwhelm her. Hold her by force if need be." Malcolm fought the desire to throttle the man. "Were you no' meant to keep her safe?"

"Aye so. Yet were we not bound to Dun Ballan all the while, with the aim of going inside?"

"She was to go in my company!"

"How was I to know—"

Malcolm fought down his rage and pain. A slaughter now would avail him nothing; these three men made up his only allies.

Yet his stomach turned within him as he asked, "And the wee lass wi' the black hair went with her?"

"Aye." Lionel seemed to view that as a good thing, for he brightened slightly. "At least she has a companion."

Indeed, a scrap of a lass. A witch. One who might well, under the right impetus, demonstrate her abilities imprudently.

Malcolm had a sudden vision of Tansy strapped to the wall of Latham's dungeon, the very place he had been, enduring the same fate. Ah, he'd saved her from the Royal Commission only to dump her in equally cruel hands.

How could he have let her come along? For the sheer pleasure of bedding her? Now look what his selfishness had wrought.

Aye, and that would teach him. He'd gone through most his life putting others before himself—his Da, his men, Mercien…even Catha. The very first time he took something he wanted, it came back on him.

And on her.

Was he willing to admit he wanted Tansy Bellrose Gant? Ah, perhaps he hadn't realized how badly until the moment she rode beyond his reach.

He swallowed down his sickness. He'd been willing to sacrifice Catha, whom he loved, for Mercien's sake—had fully intended to deceive and betray her. Why should Tansy be any different? Just because he'd held her, tasted her, felt her explode with passion in his arms?

"We will wait here for morning," he told the men. "Then I will gain admittance to the dun."

"But I gather Mistress Catha and the wee lass ha' a plan they mean to put into effect."

"Bugger that. I shall need to come up wi' one o' my own."

****

Smoke from the fire hung among the rafters of the great hall, seasoning timbers already stained dark and making the place resemble Tansy's imaginings of hell.

Not that she gave the contents of hell much thought, unless believing it might be wherever the Royal Commission sat.

Men thronged the place, mostly guards, and their number made her heart sink. A few women, presumably servants, circled among them: clearly she and Catha had interrupted supper.

And Latham himself? Tansy's eyes were drawn to a man seated not at one of the tables but in a great chair set up on a dais across the room. He lounged there as might a king, and the sight of him once more set all Tansy's instincts to howling.

Uncanny how often that now happened to her; she could scarcely remember such feelings back in Slurt. Of course, Slurt was known—safe, if she might so call it. Now she balanced on the very edge of peril.

And the disquiet she'd sensed when first laying eyes on the keep stemmed from this man, no question.

Yet he looked nothing like what she'd imagined. Not above a score and ten years, he had a burly build and dark red hair, confined in a long braid. An orange beard obscured the lower half of his face. She stood too far away to see his eyes, but his countenance did not look particularly unpleasing.

Ordinary, save for the way he made her feel inside.

She reminded herself this man had tortured Malcolm and still held his brother somewhere in the bowels of this place. God only knew how he would treat Catha.

He needed to die.

She fixed her gaze on him and repeated the thought, putting a small push of magic behind it. Aye, she'd ill-spoke Ranna in the past. That had been but practice for this.

As if in response to her ill-will, Latham got to his feet. But his gaze centered all on Catha. Tansy would wager he did not even see her.

"Mistress MacGunn." He smiled. "Well come."

The smile made Tansy want to back up a step, but she refused to admit to such cowardice.

Latham stepped down from the dais, as everyone in the room stared, and approached Catha the way a fox might track a hare. Now that Tansy saw him better, he had the look of a fox about him, a particularly well-fed fox that killed for sport rather than hunger. A very large fox indeed, for he towered over Catha and positively dwarfed Tansy. The padded tunic he wore increased his breadth, and he brought with him a scent of pure male.

His gaze, all over Catha and gloating, gleamed with avarice. "Indeed, I maun confess I did no' expect to see you here yet. I did no' expect that lack-wit Montgomery to accomplish the task I set him quite so speedily."

Catha lifted her head and straightened her narrow back. From her position, Tansy could not see her face well, but that posture spoke aloud. "Forgive me, Master Latham. I do no' ken what you mean."

"To be sure, you do not." Latham's eyes, as Tansy could now perceive, were a tawny dark brown and dangerous as murky water. "You ha' just happened by, to visit me by chance."

"No." Catha stole a look around the vast room. "I ha' come to speak wi' you, but not before all this company. May we no' be alone?"

"It is, Mistress MacGunn, the dearest wish of my heart."

"To speak, I mean."

"That may be arranged. Do you no' want some supper first? And some wine. You maun tak' wine. Never say you ha' ridden all the way from Castle Gunn alone?"

"You know very well I have not. Your guards would no' admit my men." Catha now sounded shaken. She gestured to Tansy. "And nay, I ha' no' come alone."

"Who is this, then?" Latham focused on Tansy, and she felt the impact of it like a physical blow. Again, somehow, she kept herself from stepping back. She could not abandon Catha, or their scheme.

"Mistress Gant is my companion."

Latham eyed Tansy curiously before giving a half shrug as if he found her unimportant. Fool. She would prove very important indeed to him when she achieved his downfall.

****

How would Malcolm ever endure the night? Aye, that thought had been with him many a time when Latham's men came to the cell where he was held, with their flaring torches and their instruments of pain, when Latham came with that accursed half-smile on his face, to watch. He'd asked himself the question when he hung in his chains listening to Mercien being tortured in the next cell, which had been even harder to bear. But now he paced in the darkness—free yet not free—eyeing Latham's fortress and waiting for the dawn.

A punishment this was, he had no doubt of it. This was unquestionably the return God sent him for planning to turn Catha over to Latham. Aye, and how could he have even contemplated such a thing? A woman who had trusted him from childhood, whom he admired to the heavens and beyond.

Yet...how could he have done aught else? Mercien—as his father insisted—must be his first, his only consideration. Could he leave his brother in Latham's hands to die a slow and merciless death?

And now...now he must face the loss of Tansy also.

He paced through the long hours, while Catha's men took some rest, and flagellated himself again and again. Lionel had spoken truly: if he'd always intended to escort Catha within, to trade her safety for Mercien's—this vile act of which he should have been ashamed, one Mercien would never condone—could he carp too much over the fact that Catha had taken it out of his hands, entered the keep without him and by her own will?

Aye, but Tansy...

He saw her again as he had last night, by the light of the single candle in the room they'd shared. Rearing up over him, naked but for that wealth of black hair streaming around her, and the look in her eyes: wild and wanton and...

His mind groped helplessly for the other word he sought, the one that might fit. *Tender.* There had been tenderness in the witch lass's gaze and in her touch when she coupled with him.

Now she'd gone into the very heart of danger. He knew what happened beyond those walls. Latham might value Catha too much to harm her. But Tansy?

The thought of what could befall her made him want to heave in the bushes and left him drenched with sweat.

Aye indeed, God repaid him well for seeking to betray Catha, with the exquisite pain of seeing Tansy go where she should not and imagining her fate.

For she'd gone where he could not protect her. But by all that was holy, Satan himself would not keep him from following, come morn.

Chapter Twenty

The chamber to which Tansy had been conducted looked comfortable and luxurious. Dominated by a huge bed hung with patterned draperies, furnished with several chests, a large carved wardrobe, and a padded bench seat, it surpassed even the rooms at Crag Corvan. A fire burned—no doubt lit by some poor soul of Noreen's ilk—yet Tansy felt cold to the bones, her hands like ice and her teeth ready to chatter.

This did not bode well, none of it. The instinct to which she could not help but listen, especially in times of trouble, continued to howl at her. She'd been forced to watch Catha walk away from her, in Latham's company for a private discussion, before being shut away here.

Not what either of them had intended when they hatched their scheme. They'd sworn to stick together. Already Latham had succeeded in separating them.

And Malcolm...

She tried to close her mind to the thought of him. He would have caught them up by now. Had he met Lionel and the other members of Catha's guard? How angry would he be?

Angry. He would be a different man from the one who'd held her in his arms last night, kissed her so sweetly, and made her feel like a queen. Nay, but 'twas not so—he'd made her feel no paltry queen but rather a conqueror, a claimer of his body and his passion. And his heart? She feared that had worked out far differently. Quite likely he'd claimed hers instead.

And thus she'd sought to protect him from this place where he'd suffered so terribly, and to leave him behind. Indeed, she'd softly kissed the wounds he still bore.

She assured herself, now, she'd rather endure any fate in this place than see him suffer so again. Aye now—there was resolve. She drew a breath and tried to close her mind to the possibility of him following her and Catha inside.

She did not often pray. Indeed, she could not be sure she believed in the kind of deity the Church espoused. She believed rather in the elements that made up her world, the ones she called upon when she wove her magic. The light and the dark. The fire, the water, the air; the earth that had cradled her all her days.

But she whispered a prayer now, that Malcolm would have the sense to stay where he was. If she and Catha were already lost—she for Malcolm's sake and Catha for Mercien's—let them then be lost. Malcolm need not throw his life after theirs.

Please, let him see it so.

****

"Forgive me, Sir Malcolm, but I do no' see the sense in you tossing awa' your safety and possibly your life."

Malcolm stopped pacing when Lionel spoke earnestly. With nightfall, they'd withdrawn into the forest and Malcolm could no longer see Dun Ballan even though he still felt its presence. The other two guards remained asleep, but Lionel had risen with the dawn and interrupted Malcolm's lengthy pacing.

"I suggest you get some rest and await what the day brings."

It should bring Mercien's release—if Latham had any honor, which Malcolm scarcely believed. If it happened, if Mercien emerged from the stinking hole in which he'd been held, covered in wounds, what should Malcolm do then? What could he do but conduct his brother safe away? That had been his intention ever since the moment Latham released him.

He'd been willing then to countenance trading the safety of one he loved for that of another he loved. But that had been before Tansy Bellrose Gant entered his life. How he felt about her he could not fairly say. She'd beleaguered him ever since he rode over that rise in the roadway and saw her lashed to the post. A complication he did not need. A responsibility he did not welcome. An invitation he could not bring himself to refuse.

What should he do? Wait here for Mercien? Risk himself, and perhaps Mercien in turn, by following her—them—inside? If he fell once more into Latham's hands, who would rescue Tansy, or indeed Catha, then?

Mercien must be his first concern. He owed that to his father, and to Mercien also. Catha, he argued with himself as he had from the start, would survive. Latham would not dare harm her too terribly, as his wife—if being compelled to share the monster's bed could be construed as not being harmed too terribly.

He shivered where he stood. What had he done?

The only thing he could. As for Tansy…

He turned away from Lionel and once more took to pacing.

****

"Are you well, mistress? What said he to you?" Tansy grasped Catha's hands, which felt cold as her own. Catha had been conducted to the chamber by a servant with a light. The keep now lay quiet; surely they had reached the heart of the night.

"You were gone ever so long."

"Aye." Catha's cheek looked pale, and her hands quivered. "We did speak long together."

Tansy for once held her tongue, sensing Catha needed time to marshal her thoughts before speaking further. Towing her to the bench, she compelled Catha to sit, still holding her hands.

"I hope," Catha said at last, "I ha' no' given away our intent. 'Tis a difficult thing, holding a conversation wi' that man. He has a tricky mind and sees far too much. He unsettles me." Catha's worried blue gaze met Tansy's. "I hope he did not see what lies in my heart."

"Your feelings for Mercien, you mean?" And how would Tansy conduct herself in Catha's place? If she knew Malcolm languished somewhere in this vast pile, chained and subject to tortures that left the sort of wounds she'd seen? She might well lose her mind with the desperation of it, rant and rail at Latham and completely reveal her weakness.

Catha nodded. "I wanted so badly to bargain and beg for Mercien's release, to win him free. I could no' and had to sit there listening to Latham pretend to be welcoming and accommodating. Och, he is welcoming, all right. Accommodating…I am no' so certain."

"What said he to you? And what said you o' your appearance here?"

"Just as you and I discussed. I said Malcolm had

come by Castle Gunn and let slip that Mercien is being kept here. I did no' say 'imprisoned.' I did no' dare. I told Latham that as a good friend and having known Mercien from childhood, I felt compelled to come and inquire for his welfare. I said whatever misunderstanding had led to Latham believing himself injured or insulted by Mercien maun be just that, a misunderstanding. That Mercien is the fairest and sunniest natured of men—"

Catha promptly broke down, drew her hands from Tansy's and covered her face with them. Not certain what to do, Tansy sat and watched her struggle to control her emotions, while compassion flooded her heart.

The compassion sat strangely enough—in truth, she rarely thought of anyone but herself. Not her Da, working long days to keep them fed, nor Bessie, attempting to maintain peace in the house despite Tansy's shenanigans. Now, though, she cared—far too much—about Malcolm. And Catha? Och, she could not let herself grow attached to this woman. For if things went wrong, Catha must be sacrificed.

She, Tansy, could not permit things to go wrong.

"There now," she said meaninglessly. "And how did Latham respond?"

Catha raised a devastated face from her hands. "He said Mercien maun pay the price for his disloyalty. That he had acted against the Crown in France and he, Latham, represented the King's interest. He is very high in King James's confidence, you ken."

"Aye."

"And can I question the intent o' the King?"

Tansy could. James's fierce and unreasoning stance

against witchcraft had turned the country on its head and unleashed a spate of persecution that might well have seen her sentenced to an excruciating death.

"I asked, very gently of course, why Mercien had no' been put to trial if he had committed acts against his king. Latham said he might well be, in due time, did events no' occur to change the complexion of things."

"Events?"

Catha's gaze met Tansy's. "I believe he will agree to release Mercien—eventually—if he gets what he wants. 'Tis all a ploy, this—Mercien's imprisonment, Malcolm's imprisonment and release… He wants for me to wed wi' him." Catha drew a ragged breath. "And can I do otherwise if no other persuasion serves?"

Catha seized Tansy's hands once more and leaned close in the stillness of the night. "There is but one solution; we maun act as we planned and see that monster dead."

Chapter Twenty-One

How best to kill a man? Tansy lay with her cheek on her hand and contemplated the question while gray morning light strengthened outside the dun. Aye, it had seemed a far easier proposition before she set eyes on this place—on Latham himself, and all his guards. No woman, nor likely man, would get near him with any weapon.

And that meant only magic would serve.

Magic made a dangerous prospect when it came to murder. Tansy could not be at all sure she possessed skill enough to accomplish it. Och aye, in the past she'd dabbled with using the power that lurked inside her, giving Ranna that wee push toward a mud puddle, wooing Ossian out into the dark evening, dropping a tree limb in Malcolm's path.

Causing Latham's death within his own stronghold while surrounded by his people would prove far more difficult. Tansy knew a bit about potions and poisons but would not be able to get near enough to use them by any road, though Catha might. All she had was this knowing that built inside her, the urge to influence, to push.

Could she push a man to his death?

And what of Malcolm? Could she somehow keep him from rushing headlong to join them here and so place himself in peril?

She would do near anything to keep him safe. She shifted onto her back and stared at the bed hangings while she contemplated that unsettling fact. She understood how Catha felt, why she would agree even to wed the terrifying Latham for Mercien's sake.

She glanced at the woman who lay beside her. Catha had been awake most the night, tossing and turning, but slept now, her cheek pale in the gray dawn.

Let her sleep, whispered the voice inside Tansy. Marshal your strength, explore this power within, try to discover what you can do.

Eyes wide, she probed the source of the strange ability she harbored, something she'd never done before. With the specter of her mother before her, she'd striven mostly to hide the power that often taunted and tempted her. Never had she considered its source.

But she knew it to be an ancient thing, akin to that which turned the seasons, made the trees blossom and the salmon run. Aye, akin to life itself.

How could such be a bad thing? How condemned by Church and King? How deserving of pain and fire?

For an instant, fear clutched at her throat. If she used this power—even for good—and got caught, she would face just that fate, full circle from the pillar at the crossroads. But if she failed to help Malcolm...

Again she tried to focus on the source of her power. It seemed to well up as a spring did from the ground, at the very center of her being. But what lay beyond the welling place? Was there a vast pool of magic, like the water beneath a spring that never ran dry?

What, then, might happen if she tapped into it?

She did not need to grope for the answer.

It came swift and sure.

She could kill a man. If she dared.

****

Malcolm narrowed his gaze on the dark pile of stone that comprised Dun Ballan and tried to calm the pounding of his heart. Rain poured down from a lowering gray sky and only the loyalty of Lionel and his men to Catha kept them here at the edge of the wood.

The guards in the bridge tower had been astir early, and Malcolm dared not show himself if he did not mean to seek entrance.

And he'd not yet decided on his best course of action.

Anger lingered at how Catha and Tansy together had deceived him. They must have hatched this scheme between them, to enter Dun Ballan without him. He could only ask himself why.

His heart strove to supply reasons he scarce could believe. Did they think they might succeed better without him? Did they suppose they'd protect him by keeping him from Latham's reach? He might believe that of Catha, a lifelong friend. But Tansy?

He and she had shared several nights of passion, nothing more. Aye well, there had been those moments of tenderness and the way she sometimes looked at him…but could that be enough to make such a wild lass sacrifice herself for his sake?

And what, precisely, did she and Catha intend to do? Rescuing Mercien was his mission, entrusted to him by his father. It went hard to hand it over to anyone.

"Sir Malcolm." Lionel stepped up beside him determinedly. "How long do you think we maun wait here? Do you expect Mistress MacGunn to finish her visit and emerge soon?"

Malcolm glanced into the man's worried face. "She did no' say aught to you, when she went? Did no' tell you to wait?"

Lionel shook his head slowly. "I ha' been thinking on it. She did no' in truth tell us to wait. She was just very insistent upon going in. You do think she will return?"

"I do not." He never had, from the first sickening moment he reached this place. But he did expect—hope for—Mercien.

Lionel frowned. "Do our mistress and the wee lass need us to attempt a rescue? Only, the place looks well fortified. And there are gey few of us. I have discussed it wi' the others and think we should hie back to the estate and raise a troop of household guard."

An interesting proposition. "How many could you raise?"

"Perhaps a score."

Malcolm once more turned his gaze on the keep. "Not enough."

"Aye but how can we abandon our lady?"

"We will no' abandon her. I mean to wait one more day. If our ladies are no' back wi' us, then I will mysel' call on Master Latham."

"Then, Sir Malcolm, we will wait wi' you, and the weather be damned."

****

"I am surprised, Mistress MacGunn, you ha' no' remarried, after being widowed so sadly and so soon."

Tansy shifted in her chair at the great dining table and waited for Catha to respond to Latham's remark.

Their cat-and-mouse conversation had been going on throughout the meal—which felt endless—and before the eyes of Latham's other guests, all male and as far as Tansy could tell all his cronies. They watched her and Catha the way hungry bears might watch the leap of salmon over a weir, waiting to pounce.

Unsavory characters all, yet it was Latham himself who set the warning chasing up Tansy's spine. Nearly a full day they had spent in the keep, and she'd seen him smile countless times. None of those smiles reached his eyes, which despite their warm color remained lifeless as those of a corpse.

Tansy could not imagine where Catha got her aplomb. Such self-control bespoke great inner strength, but it had now begun to fray a bit around the edges.

Her voice trembled very slightly when she said, "I canna' deny, Master Latham, there ha' been offers. Due to my bereavement, I am no' yet ready to remarry."

"Your bereavement," he repeated flatly. "You were fond o' your late husband, then?"

"A good wife is always fond of her husband, Master Latham."

"Nay, mistress, a good wife is always dutiful, no matter what is asked o' her."

Tansy shivered where she sat. She did not like the way those words rolled off Latham's tongue.

"Of course," Catha murmured and bent her head. "I am surprised you, yoursel', have no wife."

"I ha' been waiting for the right woman, one particular woman." Latham produced another of those smiles that merely bared his teeth.

"And if that woman should refuse you, after all your waiting?"

"Then I should hope to persuade her. However necessary." Their eyes met. "As, I hope, our discussion earlier did prove."

Indeed, Catha had this afternoon made what she'd called a reasoned and concerned plea for Mercien's release. She'd had no time, before dinner, to tell Tansy how that had gone.

Catha would agree to the marriage if she had to; it would then be up to Tansy to eliminate the bridegroom.

If she could.

She toyed with her food, sure she'd choke if she attempted to swallow a bite, and fixed her eyes on Latham, wondering if she could give him a push, just a wee bit of an urge to release Mercien.

Her stare centered his attention on her for the first time since they'd entered the chamber. As if he felt the impact of her regard, he fixed those dead eyes on her, and she sensed the threat, cold and yet all too personal.

"Aye," he said, "I am certain all here at this board will agree, a wife should be biddable and a servant even more so. You ha' a bonny wee servant, Mistress MacGunn—if an unusual one."

Catha looked at Tansy in alarm. She'd not expected this; indeed, they'd thought for Tansy to go nearly unnoticed until she struck.

"Ah, but Master Latham, as I ha' said, Mistress Gant is no' so much my ladies' maid—though she does, out of kindness, fulfill that role for me—as my companion and friend."

"How delightful for you. And, aye, you ha' told me, Mistress MacGunn, many things. If you ha' quite finished your supper, I suggest we withdraw once more to my study and discuss them further."

Catha trembled, but she bowed her head in assent. A breath of relief escaped Tansy as they all rose from the table and Latham offered Catha his arm.

She would escape to their chamber, strive to get her thoughts in order, and decide how best to achieve her aim—the elimination of this vile man.

She slipped from the dining room in their wake and had one foot on the bottom stair when a voice called from behind.

"Mistress Gant."

Latham. She paused and spun. All the other guests had cleared off with alacrity. Latham, however, stood in the doorway of his study, from which spilled yellow light.

"Aye, Master Latham?" She tried to make her voice soft and courteous, but her loathing for him crept in.

"I trust that you are entirely comfortable in your accommodations here at Dun Ballan?"

"Of course, Master Latham."

He stepped away from the doorway, closer to her. She could smell the spirits he'd consumed with his supper and that other, more feral scent he carried. Already standing with her heels against the bottom stair, she could not retreat and kept her gaze lowered with what she hoped passed for docility.

"And I hope you enjoyed the food you just ate."

"Aye, sir."

"I hope you are prepared, lass, to pay for it."

All the air escaped Tansy in a rush.

"Look at me," he told her harshly.

"Sir—" Somehow she met his stare. His lips twisted in a wry grimace.

"I do no' care what Mistress MacGunn says. I believe you to be a servant. And female servants in this house ha' all one additional duty. I ha' no' tried one such as you before. You look like a wild creature caught in a snare. I expect I shall enjoy mysel'."

"I will no—"

"You will, unless you want your mistress to pay the price."

Anger flared in Tansy's heart. It allowed her to meet Latham's stare fully and potently.

"Hate me if you will," he told her. "But come to my chamber as soon as Mistress MacGunn returns to yours. 'Tis that door there, at the head of the stairs. Do no' fail, or it will be the worse for you."

He turned on his heel, oblivious to the anger now burning inside her, and made his way back to the study. Tansy could not keep a shudder from wracking her body.

What to do? Tell Catha? Leave this place at once, abandoning their plans? Go to Latham's room as bidden and find a way to kill him? But they'd not succeeded in finding Sir Mercien yet.

One thing she knew for certain. She would accept no man, however bidden. None, that was, save Malcolm.

Chapter Twenty-Two

"He has laid down his demands," Catha said brokenly, sitting on the edge of the bed and trembling in every limb. "He will release Mercien, aye—but only if I wed wi' him."

Tansy hunched beside the bed and grasped Catha's fingers. The woman looked distraught, her self-composure crumbled at last. "Aye well, you knew it would be so."

Catha met her gaze ruefully. "I knew it, aye. And be certain, I would do anything—aught at all—to relieve Mercien's suffering. 'Tis as if I can feel him here in this place all the while, fair taste his agony. I maun win him free. But being faced wi' Latham full on—I will admit, it daunts me."

"I canna' blame you. What is he like, this Mercien, to inspire such loyalty—such love—in both his brother and you?"

Catha's face lit. "He is like a warm fire on a cold night, like the sun after days o' rain. He is funny and honest and bright—at least he was, before he fell into Latham's hands. What he might be now, I canna' say. I ha' loved him as long as I can remember."

"And he, you?"

"And he, me. Here is something I never told anyone else, not even Malcolm. Mercien and I plighted our troth to one another as children."

Tansy's brows flew up. "At what age?"

"I was perhaps seven—he maybe nine or so. A secret it was, but true. So when I went to my marriage, I never felt it a union in truth, you ken. I already belonged to Mercien."

"Then we maun win him free. But..."

A pounding erupted at the chamber door. Both women leaped to their feet as if prodded and stared at the panel.

"Jesu," Catha breathed. "What now?"

Tansy's skin pricked. "I am afraid I ken. When we left the dining room earlier, Master Latham demanded my attendance. In his chamber."

Catha met her gaze in horror. "Nay, Tansy. You canna'."

"How can I refuse? He said 'twould be the worse for you if I did not come to him."

"But you canna' allow him to unleash his vile appetites." Catha paled. "I did no' drag you into this only to take such abuse."

"You did no' drag me at all. I came o' my own will."

The furious knocking sounded again. Catha jerked into motion, hurried to the door, and yanked it open.

"What is it? We are trying to rest."

"Your servant is required." The footman wore absolutely no expression. "By Master Latham."

"She is no' my servant but my honored companion and will be treated as such. Tell Master Latham I need her here."

A muscle in the man's cheek twitched, and a second man appeared from the gloom behind him. Tansy knew then they had instructions to take her by force if necessary.

She stepped forward and elbowed Catha aside. "I will go."

Catha stared. "But…"

Tansy gave her a look. "Trust me."

The men seemed relieved. They led Tansy, hemmed between them, to the door at the head of the stairs. One of them knocked respectfully.

The voice from within brimmed with careless confidence. "Send her in."

Tansy grimaced. So sure, was he, that he should have what he desired this night? Aye and she didn't know quite what she would do to prevent it, but darkness gathered in her heart.

The room—large, luxuriant, and well-lit—boasted a fire and a padded settee where Latham lounged, already half unclad. He wore no shirt, and his feet were bare. His eyes met Tansy's as she walked in and the door shut behind her.

"About time," he grunted. "I bade you come at once."

"Mistress MacGunn needed me, sir." Tansy lifted her chin. "My first loyalty is hers."

Latham smiled. "As so it should be. But she will be staying here wi' me now—she and I will soon wed. And my appetites require assuagement before that time. So you see, you ha' a duty here as well."

Tansy stared at him, the blackness at her heart increasing. What a curious thing it seemed—growing in response to the ugliness in Latham, as if he prompted or even summoned it. Aye so, she'd felt a wee bit of such in the days when Ranna baited and taunted her, but naught like this.

Latham smiled again, a smug thing. "Some acts a man does no' inflict upon his wife. But a servant is far different. Remove your clothing—let me see wi' what I'll amuse mysel'."

Unmoving, Tansy continued to stare into his eyes. With his red hair loose upon his shoulders he looked even more the fox, and dangerous as a drawn dirk.

He waved a hand. "Come, unless you would feel the weight o' my fist. I wish to learn if you taste as wild as you look."

Tansy untied the laces at her bodice, her fingers fumbling over the task. Latham sat observing her every movement as she loosened the garments and shrugged from them one by one. Despite the warm air in the room, she shivered when the last of them came away.

Latham rose to his feet slowly, his gaze all over her. "Very good. Are you a virgin?"

Tansy, throat closed, shook her head.

"Just as well—I ha' no patience for weeping and wailing. If you wish to please me, you will tak' all I do wi'out complaint."

Tansy had no wish to please him. To hurt him, aye. The power inside her—black as the pit of midnight— had become a tremendous thing. Surely she could use it.

"Come here. Bend over the bench and spread your legs. Tak' your hair down first."

Tansy reached for the pins, eager to stall him any way she could. When her hair fell free, Latham gestured roughly.

"You're a tiny thing. Let us see what you can tak'."

Tansy crept forward on silent feet. She stole one look into his eyes and quickly looked away again. He seized her by the shoulder and thrust her down across the bench where he wanted her before knocking her legs apart with his foot.

Damn the man. She would have bruises on both ankles. And everywhere else he touched her, no doubt.

He would not touch her.

Upon the thought, the darkness inside her exploded. Very nearly beyond her control, it struck out at him—no wee nudge, this, nor indeed anything like she'd ever employed before. Through an enormous act of will, she curtailed it at the last instant and whispered, *Sleep.*

Latham collapsed onto the bench, nearly crashing into Tansy in the process. For an instant she stood, arms crossed over her naked breasts, and eyed him.

Dead?

Nay, for he still drew breath. He'd landed on his face, one shoulder uppermost, and breathed heavily. When Tansy could bear to touch him, she prodded him over onto his back and stared into his face.

Ah, by the powers! She'd spared herself an unspeakable ordeal, but what about when he woke and realized she'd thwarted him?

She licked her lips, tasting the power within. The shove she'd given had not required much; an abundance yet remained.

Fighting her distaste, she bent and took his face between her hands. In a low voice she whispered, "You will awake convinced you had your desire—that you did to me all you wished before you fell asleep." She let the dark power flow through her and into him, potent with her will.

She let go of him, and his head lolled back against

the bench. She gathered up her clothes and climbed into them, never taking her gaze from Latham.

Victory surged through her, along with doubt. Should she give him an extra push and try to stop his heart? Would that make it harder or easier to free Sir Mercien? Latham needed to die, aye, but perhaps not yet.

Accepting that as answer, she tied up the front of her gown and, swift as a bird, fled back to Catha's chamber.

****

"You did what?" Catha's eyes went so wide Tansy could see white around the blue before they narrowed abruptly. "You pushed him. Whatever do you mean?"

"'Tis a thing I am able to do, give folk a wee push wi' my will behind it. No matter, he sleeps and—"

"He did no' harm you?"

"I did no' give him the chance."

"But when he wakes…"

"He will think all he desired passed between us."

Catha gasped.

Tansy barreled on, "Before that happens, we maun decide—"

"Wait just a moment." Catha seized Tansy's arm and towed her to the bed, where they sat. "Are you speaking of…witchcraft?" She whispered the last word.

"'Tis no' an evil power," Tansy asserted, denying how she'd felt when she faced Latham. He had summoned something dark and strong from her, just as Ranna had sometimes summoned something hateful. "'Tis a natural strength that comes fro' the world around me that—"

"Witchcraft," Catha restated with clarity. She

released Tansy's wrist. Tansy felt the sting of disappointment; she'd dared hope she and Catha had formed a friendship. Had she just lost Catha's regard?

"So folk do name it," she admitted unhappily.

"Jesu! Does Malcolm know you possess this ability?"

"Aye. 'Twas he saved me from being sent to the Royal Commission for questioning. I told him then I was no witch. To speak true, mistress, I do no' feel like one. I wish no harm to anyone." Except sometimes. "And I speak no spells or incantations. I just…"

"Give people a magical push."

"Aye, with my will behind it."

"Such could get you burnt at the stake. Should Latham find out—"

"He will no'. I tell you, I influenced him to think he had me as he sought, and was satisfied."

"A useful skill, to be envied by any number of women."

"Do you mean to expose me, mistress?"

Catha chewed her lip. "Nay. You are far too valuable to me—to Mercien. Besides, if Malcolm saved you, well, who am I to differ wi' him? But by God, be careful. Fear runs rife in the country just now."

"I ken."

"Meanwhile—"

"Meanwhile I suggest we tak' advantage of Master Latham's condition and go exploring. Let us see if we can discover where your Mercien may be confined."

Chapter Twenty-Three

The rush light shook in Catha's hand, sending shadows leaping along the corridor. Those moving just ahead of Tansy did not seem too frightening, but when she peered back over her shoulder, she kept thinking one of the guards had followed them, and her heart pounded in her ears deafeningly.

There had been many guards. So far, she and Catha had evaded them all as they descended into the bowels of the keep, going ever deeper.

"How do you know what direction to take?" Tansy whispered at one point.

"I ha' been raised in just such a place and ken how the passageways lie. Hush and follow me."

Past the kitchens they went, past rooms piled with weaponry and old furniture, and the air grew steadily colder. Tansy wrapped her arms around herself and tried not to shiver. At last, from down a well-worn flight of steps, they heard voices, echoing up to them, and paused as one.

"What—" Tansy began.

"Hush," Catha breathed again. "Sound does carry."

She edged down the steps, her back brushing the stone wall, and Tansy followed reluctantly. The light here filtered up just like the voices and, when they crept near enough, showed them a scene.

Two men sat at a rough table, playing with a dirk,

flipping it into the air and tossing it over and over again into the scarred wood planking, playing at some contest. Both wore the garb of Latham's guards. Beyond them stretched a narrower passage, very dim. One that led to cells?

Suddenly, with all her being, Tansy wanted to flee. The feeling came from deep within, as primal as the magic she sometimes employed. She feared imprisonment in one of those cells, could taste the terror of the chilly dark.

She did not want to end up there. Nay, anything but that.

Catha placed her lips against Tansy's ear and violated her own ban against speaking. "Can you gi' them a push?"

"Eh?" Tansy gasped.

Catha's intense blue stare scorched her. "As you did Latham."

Could she? Tansy eyed the guards, very much awake and engaged with each other, talking and laughing. Two of them. She'd never attempted such a feat.

And her terror seemed to have a stranglehold on her power. With Latham, anger and hate had fueled it. Not now.

She shook her head.

Catha seized both her arms. "Please."

The movement must have caught the attention of the guard who sat half facing them. He looked up and whistled through his teeth. "Wha—"

Panic punched Tansy in the gut. If apprehended, would she and Catha be forced into one of the cells that doubtless lay beyond? Her power burgeoned in response, arising the way a war horse might to the scent of battle. She hit the man in the forehead with a bolt of will that knocked him back in his chair and made his eyes roll up in his head.

Sleep, she ordered desperately. *Sleep.*

"Eh?" His companion leaped up and turned in a baffled circle, scanning the area. Tansy and Catha, each holding her breath, pressed into the dank wall, and his gaze passed over them. He leaned down and touched the sleeping man's chest as if expecting to find a weapon embedded there. Then he looked at the dirk in his hand.

Tansy took the opportunity to push him also, far more gently than the first man. He collapsed onto the table and commenced snoring.

Catha seized her fingers and squeezed so hard it hurt. "Ah! A blessedly useful skill. Come on."

"There may be others."

"I do no' think so. How long will they sleep?"

"I do no' ken."

"Then hurry."

Tansy eyed both men as she and Catha edged past. Neither stirred, but her heart thumped wildly in her chest. Should she stay here and watch to make sure they did not awaken? Would it be safe for Catha to go on alone?

Ah, but now she could see Catha need not go far. There, in the shadows beyond, she saw three cell doors, lying just past an open grate set into the stone floor.

Catha dropped first to her knees above this, striving to peer into the cell below by the fitful light.

"Mercien? Mercien!"

Not a sound came in response. Only an evil smell

issued up from the dank place below, as indescribable as it was stomach-turning. Tansy again had an image of herself confined to such a place. It stole her breath.

"I do no' think he's there," she groaned.

"Or he canna' answer." Catha stumbled to her feet and hurried to the first of the cell doors. She thrust her face to the grate. Tansy resisted the urge to pull her back.

"I can see naught. 'Tis too dark. Mercien!"

"There." Tansy's overwrought ears caught a thread of sound. "The last door."

Catha rushed to the portal on the right. "Mercien?"

The response came in a groan. "Catha? For the love o' God—"

"Sweet Jesu! Mercien! Come to the door."

"I canna'. I canna." The faint voice sounded weak and distant to Tansy's ears, as it must have to Catha's. She seized the bars of the grate and pressed close. "Are you hurt?" She wept. "Can you no' rise? Och, but I want to touch you."

"Chained. By God, what are ye doing here?"

Catha replied, heartbreakingly, "I am here because you are."

"Go. Save yoursel'. He has broken me, Catha. Broken me."

"Nay, I will no' leave while yet you remain. Mercien, I love you. Do you hear?"

Had ever there been a braver declaration? Tansy squeezed her eyes shut against the pain and beauty of it. And the hopelessness.

Broken. She, who had seen Malcolm's wounds, need not wonder what that meant. And for all her sympathy, she could not begin to guess how they would free Mercien from that cell. Giving two guards a push was one thing, a whole keep full of them went beyond consideration.

"Help me get him out of here," Catha said over her shoulder. "There maun be a key."

"Where?" Tansy scanned the area. No keys hanging handily on the wall. None in sight on the table.

"Search the guards."

"Catha, I canna'. I do no' ken if they will wake." Terror swamped Tansy and the vision returned: hard hands on her, and being thrust helpless into the malodorous darkness. If she fell into the underground cell, would she break a limb? Lie there agonized in the stinking gloom?

"There must be a key."

"Latham carries it." Suddenly Tansy knew that for truth as if someone had spoken the words. "He keeps it on his person."

Catha stared at her. "How do you know this?"

Tansy shrugged.

Catha seized her shoulders. "Then you will have to get it from him. While he sleeps." Her blue eyes gleamed like those of a madwoman. "I canna' leave him there. Would you leave Malcolm?"

"Malcolm." The word echoed from the cell like an utterance from another world. "Say he is safe."

Catha swung back to the door. "He is. For now."

"Keep him so. Keep yoursel' so, Catha. Let me die."

Let me die.

The words smacked of defeat and struck Tansy to the heart. Where had fled the sunny, cheerful soul everyone described? Gone, gone...

She turned to the grate in the door and called, "Master Mercien, please keep strong. We will return for you. You need only hold on till then."

Mercien made no reply. Tansy seized hold of Catha, who wept copiously.

"We maun go if we're to have a hope of rescuing him later. Come."

"Mercien! Mercien, my love stays with you."

Forget, Tansy whispered to the guards as she passed them, all too aware that nothing followed them from Mercien's cell, nothing save silence.

Chapter Twenty-Four

"I wish to see your master." Suffused with worry and hate, Malcolm stood in the wan sunlight of the new morning and stared into the eyes of the guard who faced him. The man had come down from the bridge tower, a sword in his hand and insolence in his demeanor. Others, as Malcolm knew full well, peered through the openings in the stone.

The night just past, black and seemingly endless, had nearly undone him. Had Latham meant to keep their bargain, Mercien would have been released by now. Ah, but had Malcolm truly expected Latham to keep their bargain?

Fool. Now he'd placed Catha in danger and yet stood no closer to freeing his brother.

Catha and Tansy. He could scarcely bear thinking on the wee lass for fear of what might befall her in the fortress. He wanted to rip Latham apart with his bare hands. He wanted to kill, as he never had even in his fiercest battles.

But the die was cast; he'd sent Lionel and his men back to gather Catha's household guard. Fool or otherwise, he stood alone.

The guard took time to spit before he replied. "I will need to ask Master Latham what manner of scum he would ha' us admit to his dwelling."

Malcolm smiled, a smile with all his hate behind it.

"You do that, since you've no brain o' your own, and he has sapped your will."

"Wait here."

Wait. Malcolm began to hate the word. He'd waited through his duty in France, to go home, waited in that damned purgatory of a cell inside this place, waited for Mercien. He needed to know what went on within. Did Mercien yet live? Did Catha and Tansy even now carry out whatever plan they had hatched together?

He cooled his heels while the watery sunlight grew in strength around him, and his anger built. When the guard returned, he brought two other men with him.

"You will have to hand over your weapons if you mean to come in."

"Nay." Last time they'd been taken from him by force and returned only when he was released—the sword that had traveled with him to France, the same that had freed Tansy from the pillar at Slurt. Now he sneered in the guard's face. "Do you fear one man so much you maun disarm him?"

"Master Latham's orders."

Malcolm eyed the pile of black stones before him. What might he not trade for those so dear to his heart?

Fool, his mind whispered again as he handed over the sword, making no move to relinquish the dirk secreted in his boot. But his heart urged him on.

For all that, his stomach turned within him as he followed the guard across the plank bridge and into the keep. Pain lay within this place, the remembrance of horror and darkness.

He shuddered inwardly when the portcullis lowered behind him. For an instant, he was back in the hopeless dark of the cell, tasting pain and smelling his own skin sear. Then a vision of Tansy Bellrose Gant came to him, dancing before his mind's eye, silver gaze agleam. He drew a breath and walked on.

Latham chose to receive him privately, which surprised him. As he knew, the bastard loved a grand spectacle, and the members of his household, as Malcolm could hear full well when he passed the hall, were at breakfast. But the guard led him to the study where Latham liked to linger and brood.

And when it came to it, the man did not appear particularly well. The morning light flooding the room showed him in a state of half undress, and with a grayish tinge to his skin.

Had the guard roused him from his bed? Surely Malcolm did not catch the man off balance at last?

But Latham's eyes grew hard when they lit on Malcolm. He dismissed the guard with a wave of his hand before he spoke.

"Ah, Montgomery. Did you no' ha' enough the last time you stepped within these walls? Would you offer yoursel' up for more of my hospitality?"

"I ha' come to collect my brother."

"Your brother?" Latham feigned surprise and did a poor job of it.

"We had an agreement. I ha' delivered on my part of it."

"Have you, indeed?"

"You wished for Mistress MacGunn in your hands, and so she does lie."

"She does." Latham heaved himself to his feet. "And a bonus along wi' her. I maun thank you for that. I enjoyed her wee companion last night."

Tansy. Rage suffused Malcolm, searing in its intensity. For an instant he saw himself drawing the dirk from his boot and slitting Latham's throat where he stood. That would not get Mercien free, his head reminded him, even as he strove desperately to mask his reaction.

He could not let Latham see how much he cared for Tansy, dared not lend him such a weapon.

He shrugged. "A woman is a woman, aye? When it comes to it, all are much the same."

Latham's eyes narrowed. "Except for Mistress MacGunn. I am thinking you and your brother ha' held her in affection for some time."

"She is a family friend. Yet I ha' delivered her to you as promised."

"Have you?" Latham questioned it once more. "She appeared at my gate on her own."

"Summoned hence by me. Do no' split hairs, Latham. Release my brother to me, and I will be off wi' him, leaving you to both women." Over his dead body—or rather, over Latham's.

The bastard seemed to ponder it. "I maun admit I will enjoy having the wee dark lass again, until I tire of her and toss her to my guards."

Malcolm managed a shrug.

"She is no' beautiful, but there is a certain wildness I find entertaining." Latham watched Malcolm closely. Curse the man and his instincts. He had a nose for vulnerability.

"Do as you will, so long as you keep your side o' our bargain."

"A bargain, was it?"

"You ken so."

"Ah well, then I suppose I maun do as you ask. This begins a new era between us. Once I unite my lands wi' those of Mistress MacGunn, I will be one o' the most powerful men in Scotland. As such, we maun forge good relations."

Better with a snake. But Malcolm nodded blandly. He hoped his Da might live forever, but when he did pass, he, Malcolm, would inherit Crag Corvan. And he'd go to war with this man before forging ties.

"In the spirit of good will, you will dine wi' me tonight," Latham declared, "before you leave."

Malcolm grunted.

Latham's eyes gleamed. "You and your brother will dine wi' me. And, of course, the bonny Mistress MacGunn."

"You will release Mercien from your dungeon and set him at your board?"

Latham pretended to consider it. "Of course, you would perhaps first like a chance to see his wounds tended. Let me prepare a chamber and lend you the use of my dispenser—still in the spirit of good will."

"Release him, and we will be awa' from here. I will tend my brother on the road."

"I fear he will be much too weak for travel. I maun insist you stay." The word "insist" came accompanied by a gleam in Latham's eyes that screamed *threat*.

Malcolm drew a breath. What best to do? "I wish to see my brother at once."

"Then come."

****

Their descent into the bowels of the keep turned Malcolm's blood cold and brought back all the emotions he'd felt when here before—helplessness, agony, and anger so sharp he might slay the man beside him with it. Naught had ever gone harder with him than leaving Mercien here in darkness. Yet every step now stole his breath. Would Latham keep his word? Would he instead force Malcolm back into the cell, now that he had what he wanted?

Catha. And Tansy.

Had the brute hurt her? Catha, as he'd assured himself, carried a measure of protection due to her importance. Tansy possessed none. Latham might do anything to her.

But he could not let that deter him from rescuing Mercien.

The guards in the lower level met Latham's arrival with a flurry of activity.

"Bring a light," he ordered them. When the torch had been lit, Latham fished inside his tunic and produced a key. Malcolm waited in silence, heart pounding, while he applied it to the door of Mercien's cell and swung wide the door with his own hands.

The odor hit Malcolm first, thick and suffocating, bringing back the memory of suffering with such potency he gagged involuntarily. He knew full well that the only time light entered this place, pain followed, and he wished he could shield Mercien from such anticipation.

He called out, "Brother, I am here."

Stepping into the cell took all Malcolm's courage and was, he knew, a calculated risk. Latham could well slam the door on him and lock it once more. At least then he'd be with Mercien, an agony halved.

Or doubled.

The light revealed his brother then, and he forgot

everything else. Mercien hung in manacles against the stone wall, in an attitude of pain. All but naked, he wore only a stained, filthy kilt, and the floor beneath him bore spatters of his blood, as well as piss and excrement. When the light found him, he raised his dark head, and Malcolm gasped again.

"By God! What ha' you done to him?"

"There was a small mishap during one o' our…sessions. The iron slipped."

Malcolm turned from the unbearable sight of his brother and launched himself at Latham, the sheer impetus taking them both over onto the filthy floor. The hard hands of the guards plucked him off. More men rushed in from outside to subdue him, and Latham, an ugly look on his face, scrambled up.

"I will excuse you that," he said, "as your emotions are stirred." To his men he added, "Get him out of the shackles and bring him upstairs."

"Nay." Malcolm barked the words. "No one touches my brother—no one but me."

Chapter Twenty-Five

"I will kill him."

Malcolm uttered the words—a vow—as he leaned over the bench upon which his brother lay stretched, in the dispensary. He'd sent the dispenser away, a man he remembered all too well from his visits to the cell down below, determined to tend Mercien with his own hands. Versed in providing rough care in the field, he could do so well enough—all save that one injury upon which he could scarcely bear to look.

"You should no' be here, brother," Mercien spoke in a weak voice, rough with pain. "You were well awa'. Why return?"

"You ken why." Malcolm smoothed the filthy hair back from Mercien's face tenderly. "You were here."

"Aye so, and I canna' fault you. I would ha' done the same for you. Yet now there are two o' us trapped…again. And worse—I thought I heard Catha's voice outside my cell."

Malcolm wrung out the already stained cloth in the basin and laid it to a burn on Mercien's shoulder. He said nothing.

"I may ha' imagined it," Mercien rasped. "I ha' imagined many and many a thing while hanging there against that wall. I imagined Mother came to me, and she how many years dead?"

"Too many."

"Tell me Catha is no' here. Brother, say you did no' give in to that bastard's demands and fetch her to him."

Again Malcolm kept silent.

"Brother!" Mercien reared up, anger giving him the needed strength. "I endured all I did for her—to keep her safe."

"I could no' leave you here, Mercien. You could no' expect it."

"You should ha' respected my wishes. You ken fine what she means to me."

"Aye." Malcolm swallowed convulsively. "She means much to me also. But you—"

"I am already lost."

"Nay." Instinctively, Malcolm denied it. "Nay."

A terrible smile twisted Mercien's lips. "How bad is it, Brother? Look me in the face and tell me."

Bad. But Malcolm could not tell him that; he did not want Mercien to give up.

Instead he asked, "When—?"

"No' long after you were released."

"Why? He already had what he wanted."

Mercien smiled his terrible smile again. "Why? Need you ask? The man enjoys it. List to me, Malcolm. Is Catha truly here? If so, if you gave in to his demands, we canna' leave her in that monster's hands. Tell me now—"

The door of the dispensary crashed open, and a fair-haired blur flew past Malcolm. Clad in a blue gown, it fell to its knees at the side of the bench where Mercien lay.

"Mercien! Och, Mer—"

Catha's voice died the instant she looked into

Mercien's face. "Och, Jesu, sweet Jesu—what—"

"Is it so terrible bad, Catha? Am I so ruined you canna' look at me?"

"I am looking. Do you no' see that I am looking, my bonny boy? Och, what has he done to you? God will mak' him pay, Mercien, my love. God will—"

"I am no' sure I still believe in God." Mercien reached out a dirty, scraped hand, the marks of the shackles livid at the wrist, and touched Catha's fair hair like a man in a dream. "He did no' accompany me into that cell. But an angel is here wi' me now."

Malcolm's throat closed. He glanced over his shoulder; Tansy slipped into the room on silent feet and shut the door behind her.

Catha put her forehead against Mercien's shoulder and wept. Mercien, abandoning his weakness, drew her close and laid his lips to her hair.

A whisper of a touch on Malcolm's arm captured his attention.

"Leave them," Tansy bade, and drew him to the door.

Malcolm bent his gaze on her. "Are you bad hurt, mistress? Latham said—well, he said he forced you." Why mince words now?

"Me?" She tossed her black head. "I can tak' care o' mysel'. But your brother…" She drew a breath and said, hushed, "Latham put his eye out."

The rage licked up through Malcolm again. "The bastard claims 'twas but an accident."

"Never."

"We are agreed."

"The man is a monster. An abomination. He needs to die."

"Agreed again. But above all else I maun get Mercien awa' out of here. I ha' already failed him once."

"You have no'."

"Indeed, and there lies the proof o' it. My bonny brother, bonny no more."

"She will no' care for it. He is everything to her, and still bonny in her sight." Tansy's gaze met Malcolm's. "Love does no' look wi' the eyes, by any road, but wi' the heart."

And what did he see in her eyes? Clear as water they looked, even in the muddy light, and guarding no secrets. He could see her desire, aye, and her courage. So much braw courage in a wee lass... Did he see something more? The memory of the nights they had twined together in passion?

Tenderness.

He said brokenly, "I do no' want to leave you here—nor Catha. But I maun get Mercien awa'. Especially now. I do no' ken how he has endured so long."

"I understand."

"But lass..." He seized her hands. "I will come back for you." He would, as if drawn by enchantment.

She nodded. "Tend your brother now. I fear Catha has revealed her weakness to Latham in full by coming here. But I could no' hold her. I would no'. Seeing him may give her the strength she needs in the days to come."

"Sacrifice," Malcolm said softly. "He gave himself trying to spare her, and she sacrifices now for him. Sacrifice, and love."

****

177

"We are set to leave come morning," Malcolm delivered the words to Tansy baldly when she opened the chamber door to him, and her heart sank. He'd roused her from her bed where she'd known nothing of sleep, dreading this very announcement. Now, deep in the night, the keep seemed unusually quiet, no guards to be seen. She seized Malcolm's arm and towed him into the room.

Visibly stirred, he continued to speak as he came. "I wished to tell Catha the news. It took hours of persuasion to force Latham's cooperation. I just came from him—where is she?"

"With Mercien, of course. I could no' haul her awa'." Tansy tasted her own pain. "If this be their last night, let them spend it together."

Malcolm stilled, and his eyes met hers. Dark as the night itself his eyes were, and unfathomable. If he left come morning—as he must—it would tear her apart, draw her heart from her chest, and wound her down to the soul.

He whispered, "I hate leaving you here. Come awa' wi' me, Tansy."

"And abandon Catha?" Once she would have, without a backward glance. She'd been all selfishness then, all about what mattered to her, and hang everyone else in her world.

Now she discovered, to her surprise, that had changed. She'd forged a bond with Catha, almost as strong as that with this man.

"Latham would no' let me go. 'Twould endanger your escape wi' Mercien. Besides," she whispered before Malcolm could protest, "Catha and I ha' a mission to accomplish."

"A gey dangerous one." He caught her shoulders between his hands. They felt warm; his long session with Latham must have overheated him, for Tansy could feel heat streaming off him, and the collar of his shirt lay open, revealing a glimpse of black hair.

Aye, she knew what lay beneath Malcolm Montgomery's clothing—had touched every part of him with hands and tongue. The memory of it rendered her weak for an instant.

She leaned closer, as helpless to keep from it as to stop breathing. "I will follow after you, if I can. That I do promise."

He kissed her, an answer to the prayer that had haunted her all night long. His lips claimed hers with a hunger that bade her open to him; joy and grief tangled together inside her as his tongue possessed her mouth.

Would this be the last time she kissed him? Tasted him? Touched him? Emotion filled her to bursting, and she poured it into him, weaving as she did a spell of magic. For several glorious moments they soared together before Malcolm broke the kiss and buried his face in her neck.

Raggedly he gasped, "Tansy, wee one, I do no' ken how to part fro' you."

She gave him the only words she possessed, in return. "Then stay wi' me, for whatever time we ha' left, till morning. 'Twill no' be long, but stay. One last night."

"I should go."

"Give Catha and Mercien this time together." She gazed into his eyes. "And us."

"And us," he echoed before he slipped her nightdress over her head.

Chapter Twenty-Six

What constituted happiness? Tansy asked herself that question even as she lay beneath the ministrations of Malcolm's caressing tongue, as he parted her thighs with long, gentle fingers and entered her with a reverence that spoke of something more than passion. It seemed she'd been striving to answer that question all her life. And now, this man came to her with his bright sense of honor, his heavy duty, his scarred yet beautiful body. He rode her and claimed her, black hair flowing back from his forehead and eyes aflame, and she reached for something so priceless and complete she scarcely dared believe in its existence.

This made happiness; Malcolm did. But like all else in life, she feared the state must be fleeting. They might have only this one night to last forever.

So she whispered to him, not just with her tongue and lips but with her heart and the magic that rested at her soul. She unthinkingly wove another spell to bind them, hoping it might endure even if they never saw each other again.

Unbreakable.

The finest use to which she'd ever put her magic, an enchantment so delicate and heartfelt it left her trembling even after he'd emptied his seed inside her and lay gasping in her arms.

"Tansy," he breathed.

Should she tell him how she loved him? For that certainty now possessed her, even as the enchantment held him—nay, held both of them. She'd never imagined loving anyone as she did this man, with fire and terrifying need.

Perhaps, she thought as she spread her palms across his sweated back and caressed him gently, she'd always known instinctively how frightening love must be. It balanced perilously on a fulcrum, the other end of which was loss. Hadn't she seen that truth every time her mother's name came up and she beheld the look in her father's eyes?

Her father cared, aye, for Bessie. But he still loved her mother, Bellrose, who'd fled him and the life they shared. Or had she but fled this all-claiming intensity?

For the first time Tansy wondered, and felt an odd kinship with the woman she could not recall.

"Tansy." Malcolm breathed her name so softly it barely stirred the magic that enfolded them. She realized she could see him more clearly than when they began loving. Morning light crept through the window—their night very nearly flown.

"Aye?" She brushed her lips across his cheek rough with beard, and closed her eyes the better to absorb the sensation.

"What ha' you done to me?" The question held no accusation but a kind of yearning wonder. He too felt how their world had changed.

"I ha' but loved you, Sir Knight." As close as she dared come to the truth. Would he understand?

He lifted himself from her, shoulder muscles rippling, and gazed into her eyes. "More than that." He cupped her face tenderly. "You are a beautiful, enchanting, and vexing wee thing that will no' leave my mind—like a song, the words running over and over again. Promise me something."

"Anything," she vowed rashly, caught by the light in his eyes.

"Promise we will be together again—even though we maun part this morning. Even though I travel far awa' from you. Promise a time will come when you lie beneath me like this again and I gaze into your eyes, when I feel the woman you are."

Tansy's breath hitched in her chest. "Can you feel me?"

"Och, aye—from that wild mind o' yours right down to your toes."

Ah, and in binding him to her had she also opened herself to him? But she did not mind. She would offer this man anything, including her very life.

"If you believe you know me, Sir Knight, and want me yet—well, that is something no one else has ever done."

"I want you, Tansy Bellrose. Whatever comes between."

"Then I give you your promise. We will be together again—come what may. I will find you. Or you will find me. So mote it be."

"If you ha' bound it in magic, wee enchantress, I believe it." And he buried his face in her neck while the dawn came.

****

The ache born in Malcolm's chest early that morning when he lay in bed with Tansy refused to ease. Instead, while he saw Mercien prepared for transport and guarded against any treachery from Latham, it increased until he feared he might be dying.

Only now, when they stood ready to leave with Latham standing by, watching their every move like a spider, and among a small army of guards, did Malcolm grasp the truth. The pain he felt came from his heart being ripped out of his chest and given over into Tansy's keeping.

He feared for her, just as he feared for Catha, who had, indeed, shown her hand by her concern for Mercien. Even now, while they prepared for departure, tears stood in Catha's eyes, and her gaze clung to Mercien's every move.

Malcolm half—nay more than half—expected Latham to use that against her, demand that Mercien stay so he might compel her obedience. The arrogant bastard probably believed he needed no such threats against a defenseless woman.

Two defenseless women.

Malcolm's gaze returned helplessly to Tansy, where she lingered at Catha's back. She looked like naught so much as a waif, with her feet bare and all that black hair hanging loose down her back.

Mercien touched Malcolm on the arm. He'd insisted on donning all his clothing—though Malcolm could not imagine how he bore the garments over his wounds. The dispenser had bound a stark white bandage over the place where his eye had once been, and cleaned him up, though grime still lay embedded in his skin. No matter—he declared himself able to walk from the keep and to ride away after.

Malcolm had his doubts. He'd seen his brother, aye, endure the worst battles, seen him fight while bearing grim wounds. He'd known Mercien to ride a day and a night only to battle at the end of it. But he'd been close enough to where Mercien now stood to taste his weakness, his bone-deep pain. He knew how the wounds chafed beneath the cloth, could imagine the grief.

Pride might get Mercien away out of Latham's keep. Enduring the journey home could prove another matter.

Home. Away from Catha, from Tansy. He could not…

The pain in his chest clenched hard as he offered Mercien his arm. "Come, we maun awa'."

This would be the moment when Latham reneged, if he meant to—called them back from the edge of hope. So had he done time and time again during questioning, letting Malcolm believe the session in pain had ended, only to begin again.

"Go with God," Catha said.

"May the angels bless and keep you," Mercien told her, his heart in his voice.

The guards raised the portcullis and freedom beckoned. Malcolm remembered how he'd felt riding from here last time, leaving Mercien in chains. This felt no better now, but he must get Mercien away home to Father.

He looked at Tansy Bellrose Gant. He should have told her how he loved her when he had the chance— loved her with a deep need that surpassed mere affection.

Did she know? What did he see in her eyes?

He turned away, Mercien's weight heavy on him, and stepped toward the daylight.

A whisper touched his mind, the merest hint of

sensation. Or was it the memory of a word?
Love.

Chapter Twenty-Seven

"I should never ha' left her."

Mercien's words, spoken bitterly and not for the first time, echoed those lurking in Malcolm's mind. Now many miles from Dun Ballan, and with the day bright around them, he felt little relief. Instead he carried the pain in his chest still, an ache cold as stone lodged beneath his heart.

"We had no choice," he stated far more harshly than he intended, and eyed his brother with misgiving.

He'd been a fool to send Catha's men away to fetch reinforcements. Now the two of them rode alone, Mercien on a horse given by Latham.

Malcolm wondered how he stayed on its back, and just what he'd do if Mercien succumbed to his weakness and tumbled off. Only sheer will kept the lad there. That and the hard emotions filling him.

Those, Malcolm understood far too well.

"She told me her love for me would sustain her." Mercien shot his brother a lopsided glare. Despite the bandaging, Malcolm could barely look into his brother's face, so changed he mightn't have known him if they had met elsewhere. Mercien, the bright, shining one, the laughing one—gone. What would Da say?

"Did she, so?" Compassion flooded Malcolm and softened his tone. "A braw thing, that, to carry wi' you."

He should have given words of love, aye, to Tansy, and should have sought them from her also. Something to guard against the emptiness and battle the pain.

"Latham will compel her," Mercien's voice dripped venom. "He will force his devil's spawn on her. She will live out her days wallowing in the poison of that place."

For an instant, Malcolm could not breathe.

"Brother," Mercien grated, "let us go back."

"And do what? Take on Latham and all his men? We would no' get through the gates. Nay, let us get you home and tended. I will gather father's men and go back, make an attempt to free them."

"Them?" Again Mercien looked at him.

"Catha. And her companion."

"Her companion—the wee, dark lass. Brother, what is she to you? Is she more than Catha's servant?"

"I brought her to Crag Corvan, and before that I rescued her from a crowd o' villagers bent on seeing her tried for witchcraft."

"Witchcraft! No ordinary servant, then."

"No servant at all. I doubt anyone could constrain that lass's heart to obedience."

"Save you?"

"Eh?"

"I wondered at how you looked at her. And she at you. Ha' you bedded her?"

"An honorable man does no' speak of such things."

"He tells his brother, especially a brother desperately in need o' distraction."

"I've bedded her." If what had taken place between him and Tansy could go by so paltry a description. Surely more than mere pleasure and release had followed. He'd given part of himself into Tansy's keeping and acquired this damned ache at his heart.

Mercien fell silent for a moment before he asked, "And do you love her?"

This time Malcolm's silence seemed to provide an answer, for Mercien grunted and went on, "Then she maun be a singular woman indeed. For I've known you to love nae woman—save Catha, and that like a sister."

So Mercien might well think. Malcolm's feelings for Catha had been far more than brotherly, but they paled in comparison to what he felt toward Tansy. God help her. The prayer trailed from his mind like the steam of their breath in the chill air, even though, like Mercien, he could no longer claim unwavering belief in that deity.

He did, however, believe in Tansy Bellrose Gant.

****

"I should no' waste my strength in tears—I know that full well," Catha whispered brokenly. "I canna' seem to help it, though."

Tansy made no answer. Alone in the chamber they were meant to share, the two women huddled near a fire that failed to warm either of them. Following Malcolm and Mercien's departure, Catha had somehow held onto her poise while with Latham. But once she escaped to privacy, she'd crumbled and collapsed in Tansy's arms.

"Go on and weep," Tansy told her now. "Mayhap it will help."

"Naught will help, I fear! Do no' mistake my meaning—I am that glad to see him awa'. I kept fearing all the while Latham would change his mind or—or call them back." She raised a stricken face from Tansy's shoulder. "You do no' think he will, do you? Send a troop after them and drag them back?"

The very idea made Tansy's stomach turn. Being marooned here might be a terrible fate, but seeing Malcolm and Mercien imprisoned would be far worse. Like Catha, she clung to the thought of them free.

Who knew love would spawn such sacrifice? Especially in the breast of one such as she.

"What said Latham when you met wi' him?" The bastard had called Catha immediately into his presence as soon as the two knights rode away.

Catha whispered her answer, as if the walls had ears. "He speaks already of our marriage. He will send today and request a reading of the banns. Till then, I believe he will no' touch me—other than a kiss or a mauling." Catha shuddered. "He will allow no questions about the legitimacy of any son I give him. 'Tis greed drives him in this, rather than lust. That is…" Catha choked and paused. "I fear he will expend his lust on you. He asks already that I send you to him."

"Now? In broad daylight?" And with Malcolm barely out of her sight. How could she muddy his precious memory with Latham's vile presence?

"What will you do?" Catha asked.

Tansy gave her a meaningful look. "You ken full well."

"But how? And when?"

"Managing it will be no easy feat. And I would no' wish to act before I believe Malcolm and Mercien far enough away, just in case somewhat does go wrong." Tansy puffed out a breath. "I shall have to stall him."

"Again? What if he catches on?"

"Then I will ha' to endure whatever punishment he hands down." Could memories of Malcolm save her—

imagining herself in his arms, aflame beneath his kisses, willing to offer anything?

She didn't know and felt suddenly so ill she doubted she could rise from the bench where she and Catha huddled together.

"If he touches me," she said suddenly, "I will surely vomit."

Catha's hands tightened on hers. "Do not go to him."

"And reveal our hand?"

"We will think of something else."

"There is naught else."

"Och, Jesu! Tansy—"

Tansy freed her hands from Catha's and struggled to her feet. Courage she never knew she possessed carried her out the door of the chamber, down the stairs, and to the closed door of Latham's study, where she knocked.

How far would she go to buy Malcolm more time? Just as far as she must.

Chapter Twenty-Eight

"Remove your clothing—all of it." Latham demanded, even as he had last time. Eyes agleam, he spoke from the large chair where he lounged in defiance of the energy Tansy could feel inside him. Tansy shivered, and her eyes darted around the room, seeking escape. Sunlight, cold and clear, flooded the chamber through the two floor-to-ceiling windows overlooking a courtyard. She wondered if men passing through that space might peer inside and watch what took place, and whether they'd dare.

She had never considered herself particularly modest and had been eager enough to shed her clothing in front of Ossian. Now, however, the expression in Latham's eyes—cruel and avid—caused her to freeze where she stood.

He waved a hand impatiently. "Come, did you no' hear me? You were biddable enough before."

"Aye, Master."

Tansy thought of the fathoms Malcolm might put between himself and the keep while she distracted this monster, and reached for her laces. "I just wondered if I might no' be cold."

"There is a fine fire burning. And I mean to keep you far too busy to chill."

He watched her through slitted eyes while she loosed her bodice and dropped her skirts.

"Now tak' down that hair. I like to see it loose around you."

Tansy obeyed, grateful for any cover.

"The last time you came to me," he mused, as her fingers worked the pins, "I mounted you like a bitch in heat and found it pleasing. Did it please you also, lass?"

Tansy's mind darted, even as her eyes had. How clever and powerful a magic, that could make him believe he'd done what he wished and had what he'd had not! For an instant, she felt unusually impressed with herself.

But dared she attempt the same again?

When she stood clad in nothing but her hair, Latham crooked a finger, summoning her closer.

"Tell me, lass, ha' you ever taken a man into your mouth?"

Tansy stared as her skin flushed in mortification. Sudden memory swamped her—that of welcoming Malcolm's hot, silken strength between her lips. But she would not admit that to this man, and the lie came easily. "I am sorry, Master, I do no' believe I understand."

His impatience increased. "Pleasuring him wi' your mouth, and accepting his seed."

Tansy shook her head violently, though her lips had been all over Malcolm, including that wondrously hard length of him. She could not imagine such an act in relation to this man. "Nay!" She denied it. "People do no'—"

"I assure you, women do. And you will, if you ken what is good for you." He flipped aside the folds of his kilt and revealed that he jutted up, fully aroused.

Tansy's stomach lurched, bringing up the little bit

of food she'd taken this day, into the back of her throat. "I canna'."

"You can. On your knees, lass, here before me."

She told him with scrupulous honesty, "I will vomit."

Their gazes met in a moment of silent contest before he growled, "I care no' what you do after, so long as your mouth be hot and welcoming first. Or perhaps you would rather feel the lash on your naked back?"

"Nay."

"Then on your knees, I say." Not willing to await obedience, he lunged forward, seized her hair, and twisted his handful of it into a knot. Tansy cried out as the pain of it brought her to her knees in the required position.

And she could smell him, a rank, heavy scent of unwashed male animal. In days now well gone, Ossian had smelled good to her—like sawdust and, occasionally, horses. And Malcolm—well, his scent served to inflame her, to set her alight. This made the sickness flood her mouth and caused her to choke it back desperately.

"Please, Master..." Could she even reach for her magic from this place, subjugated and nearly helpless?

She stared up into his face, now looming above her. Cruelty warped his features; his eyes gleamed with malice and anticipation.

"Get busy. And put your throat into it."

Horror drenched Tansy with renewed heat. She took one dismayed look at his manhood, rearing up at her lips, and closed her eyes, seeking her power, summoning it like dark light.

It came with a hum, softly at first. It whispered and moaned and bubbled up; she reached for it frantically even as Latham, unwilling to wait, pulled her by the hair, closer to his groin.

At the touch of his flesh on her cheek, her power exploded. She felt it rush like a gout of fire to dry kindling, all too swiftly beyond her control. The strength of it allowed her to jerk away from him; once more they stared at one another and as they did the color drained from his face.

Tansy did not know what he saw in her eyes, but quite plainly he beheld something. The desire to murder? The fire of her rage? The power that filled her?

Whatever it was spurred him. He could not readily rise with her kneeling on his feet, but he shoved up against the back of his chair, and a single word issued from his lips—first as a whisper and then as a hoarse groan—

"Witch. Witch!"

"Nay." Tansy scrambled off his feet and backed away from him, as terror hit the pit of her stomach. Caught still in the snare of his gaze, even as he seemed caught in hers, she could not flee. He, too, froze; they stared, connected in a moment of pure communion.

She could feel his darkness, the cruel edge of the hate that lay at his heart. Could he then feel the extent of her power and the contrasting uncertainty?

He sucked in air, recovering first from his paralysis, and bellowed, "Witch! Guards, here to me!"

Tansy hit him between the eyes with her power, punching out with it as she might her fist, her aim true. Always in the past had she persuaded and suggested, or at the most, pushed. She'd never conceived her power might become so strong a weapon.

Latham fell back into the chair, his eyes rolling up in his head. But the alarm had been given; already Tansy could hear hurrying footsteps outside the room. She wanted to flee so badly she could barely breathe for it; she also wanted to cover her nakedness.

No time. She snatched up her clothes—or most of them—and tore open the chamber door, almost stumbling into the first of the guards answering Latham's summons.

Startled, the man—and his companion hurrying after—stepped back. Tansy shoved between them and, her hair trailing her, made for the stairs, where she hesitated.

Should she go to Catha or try to make her way out the main doors? But nay, they now stood filled with more guards, and the wooden bridge and watchtower the same, beyond. And she naked as the day.

She hurtled up the stairs, wondering if she but raced into a trap.

****

"List to me, Tansy. List! Do you think you killed him? Is he dead?"

It seemed to be the main question on Catha's mind; she'd already repeated it twice. The two women sat half-crouched on the bed in their chamber, Tansy wearing only her chemise, tears running down her face.

When had she commenced weeping? She rarely wept and prided herself on resisting such weakness. But she palmed her wet cheeks before she replied. "I do no' ken. He fell back—I do no' ken."

Catha raised her golden head, seeming to listen to the commotion beyond her door—plenty of commotion that penetrated even the stout oaken panel. Raised voices and more pounding footfalls; the slamming of a door.

She pondered and said, "God willing, you ha' slain the bastard. And we maun leave here before the keep recovers. Don your clothing in layers—all you wish to take. And bind your hair—it will garner far too much attention like that."

Tansy hurried to obey, hands shaking and stomach roiling. "Do you think we can get awa'?"

"I am no' certain, but we will try."

"The portcullis. And the bridge—"

"Both well-guarded, aye. Can you swim?" Catha asked the question while donning her own garments and confining her hair.

"A wee bit." Tansy did not like water.

"'Twill ha' to do. I swim like a trout, me, and will help you."

"You never mean to attempt a swim to shore? But 'tis cold out. We will tak' our deaths."

"No more dangerous than staying here, then." Catha gave Tansy a meaningful stare. "Look you—if Latham lies dead, his men may be in too much disarray to pursue us swiftly. If not, and he remembers what happened—"

Tansy hissed between her teeth. "Curse it! I forgot."

"Forgot?"

"To whisper the word 'forget.' I was so frighted..."

"And no wonder."

"He spoke the name 'witch.'" She'd already shared this truth with Catha; it bore repeating.

"Then come."

Catha opened the chamber door, and the noise from downstairs increased. Men shouted; some called loudly for the dispenser. All the furor remained, so far, at the foot of the stairs.

Catha seized Tansy's arm. "Swiftly, now."

"We will never get past there."

"We will not try. This way; there must be another stairway down."

With Catha's hand locked around Tansy's wrist, the two women sidled down the dim hallway, encountering no one. They had taken a score of steps before Tansy froze.

"What is it?" Catha breathed.

"Did you hear that?"

"What?"

"I thought I heard his voice from below. Latham."

Catha stared at her, aghast.

Tansy's eyes once more flooded with tears. "Curse it all. I hoped I had succeeded in killing him."

Chapter Twenty-Nine

"Lass!" Catha seized Tansy with both hands and shook her. "You canna' fall apart on me now."

"But he—"

"Perhaps you did no' hear what you thought you heard. Come."

They went on more swiftly now, as the commotion downstairs increased.

Tansy sought to reason it out. "But if they called for the dispenser—"

"Hush!"

The activity below seemed to have drained the rest of the keep of its occupants. When the back stairs opened at their feet, they were silent and deserted. Catha towed Tansy down, past the open doorway of the kitchen where female servants had gathered and stood gossiping, and thence through a twisting corridor to a doorway, where she paused.

"'Twill be bright daylight out there," she cautioned Tansy. "We will easily be seen. Are you prepared to slip into the water? We canna' tarry."

"Aye." But Tansy did not feel certain. Part of her wanted to go back and see whether Latham yet lived— if she'd slain a man, however deserving. Part of her feared the water almost as much as capture. Part of her had always feared deep water. Yet her choices were few.

She whispered a spell as Catha eased the door open and peered out. "Jesu! 'Tis a meeting place for the guards. Many of them are gone, and the loch lies just beyond. How fast can you run?"

"Fast." Of that, Tansy felt certain.

"Then there is no use in stealth. When I bid you, run."

"Aye." But the word lodged in Tansy's throat even as sunlight blinded her eyes. Catha towed her out the door, breathing the word into her ear rather than shouting:

"*Run.*"

Sudden shouting came from behind them, a sharp hue and cry accompanied by more pounding footsteps. They were seen! Tansy beat Catha to the water—no need of a fortress wall here—where she balked like a recalcitrant pony.

The water, cold and green, lay edged with jagged rocks, past which she must leap to save her skin. Her heart wanted to jump; her feet remained rooted to the soil.

Voices roared behind them, and Catha seized her arm again.

"Jump!"

Catha leaped, pulling Tansy with her. To avoid the waiting rocks, Tansy jumped with all her strength. They hit the water and—

For several moments, Tansy's mind lost all comprehension. Cold and terror stole the capacity for rational thought. She plunged deep into the greenness, took a breath of it, and started to drown.

She felt Catha's hand pulling at her skirts, towing her in the other direction. They broke the surface into chilly air, and she choked as water spilled out of her.

"Och, Jesu!"

Somehow Catha began to stroke, towing Tansy's nearly dead weight, struggling and straining. None of the guards, whom Tansy could just see when she rolled her eyes, jumped in after them. But their voices followed, some calling orders, and Catha groaned.

"Help me, Tansy. They mean to cut us off at the shore."

Tansy, galvanized, began to flail and splash. She could see men hurrying around to the place toward which Catha towed her.

She gasped, "Leave me. Save yourself."

"I will no'." Catha's face, white from the cold, appeared before Tansy's eyes, blue gaze beseeching. "Do no' ask it of me."

"But they—" Tansy foundered and almost went under; Catha hauled her up again.

"You maun live for Malcolm, as I maun for Mercien. Do you no' wish to see him again? Touch him, kiss him?"

"Aye."

"Then help me. Gi' them a push."

"What?"

"Use your strength—your true strength."

Weak, terrified, and drained by the cold, Tansy considered it.

The men on the shore began to shout, "Witch! Drown, witch!"

They commenced throwing stones, one of which narrowly missed Catha. A shout came from the wooden bridge, and the stones stopped flying.

Tansy knew then—Latham lived still.

"Come. Big breath."

Catha towed Tansy under the water and off on another tangent. Tansy's ears filled with icy water, her nostrils with the scent of the loch which, to her, smelled like death. Her lungs wanted to burst. She was dying.

They surfaced farther down the shore in the shelter of a snag that reared up out of the water. Tansy, gasping for breath, imagined they had but moments.

"Out." Catha thrust Tansy upward with inhuman strength. Tansy scrabbled for a hold on the shore, thrashing her wet skirts wildly and listening for any hint of discovery.

"Here, help me!"

With a grunt, Tansy hauled Catha from the water. The cold air bit at her, and she shivered violently.

"Away. Run."

No other words passed between them for some time. They'd surfaced adjacent to a stand of trees, and Catha led the way, twisting and twining between the trunks. Tansy could hear no sounds of pursuit, could hear nothing for the breath rushing in her lungs. Even the snapping of twigs underfoot became lost.

At last Catha dragged her to a halt and hissed, "Listen."

Tansy, gasping, strove to hold her breath. "Are we awa'? Are we safe?" She could scarcely believe it.

But Catha gave a sharp shake of her head. "They come."

"I canna' hear—"

"Whisht!" Catha stared into Tansy's face, her eyes full of terror. "Run!"

****

The pressure provided by Catha's hand on the back

of Tansy's neck pressed her face into the damp ground. It had started raining some time ago, adding to the misery of their flight, and Tansy suspected that made them easier to track.

Now afternoon drew on—night would soon fall. Tansy hoped if they could defy capture till then she might call the dark to cover them. But their pursuers followed mere steps behind, among the trees.

She might hold her breath but couldn't halt the deep shudders that shook her body, prompted by the cold. Suddenly she felt convinced they would be caught—knew it to her toes.

But Catha eased down on top of her, pressing her farther into the wet ground and keeping her still.

"This way!"

She could hear the men calling to one another, then the approaching thunder of their footsteps, the jingle of their weapons. She heard them push through the copse in which she and Catha had gone to ground, the snapping of twigs, and she heard their breath, hoarse and labored as her own.

"There!"

All her blood ran cold—colder than before— though little heat remained in her body. Spent, she had no time to pray or cast a spell before Catha's weight flew off her, and hard hands hauled her up after.

Two of Latham's guards, both obviously enraged, were swiftly joined by two more, who came hurrying after—not the man himself, thank all that was holy.

Not yet.

Catha gasped and began to exclaim. "Take your hands from me! How dare you manhandle me this way? Do you no' ken I am betrothed to your master?"

"Aye," returned the man who held her, Tansy having been collared by the second guard. "And that is why I dare no' leave go of you, lady. 'Tis worth the skin o' my back."

Catha exchanged a wild look with Tansy. She no longer looked like the composed, immaculate woman Tansy had first met—face and hands smeared with mud, skirts filthy, soiled blonde hair hanging down.

She lowered her voice and said to the guard, "Let us go, and I will mak' it worth your while. All of you. Accompany us awa' to Castle Gunn. I ha' great wealth and will mak' something o' you."

The man eyed Tansy. "And this one, lady? Master do say she be a witch."

Catha's gaze touched Tansy's again before she declared bravely, "She comes wi' us or we do no' go."

The man shook his head. "The land be rife wi' witches just now. Master will ken what to do wi' this one. Careful wi' her now, Archie, that she does no' cast her eye on you."

The brute holding Tansy tightened his grip painfully and cinched her higher, causing her to lose what little breath remained in her body, and making it impossible to reach for her magic.

"I ken fine," the man grunted. "The wee bitch will do no harm to me."

Chapter Thirty

"You broke your promise to me, Mistress MacGunn. And I do no' like folk who break promises."

Latham glared at Catha from his seat in the study, behind the big desk. Tansy, still held in the grasp of her captor at Catha's side, half numb and unable to stand on her own, caught the edge of that glare and marveled that Catha withstood it.

Catha sucked in a breath but said nothing. Tansy wondered if, like her, Catha searched instinctively for weaknesses in their opponent. Latham did not seem…aright. Tansy had hit him with a powerful push of magic, as evidenced by the livid red mark still visible between his eyes. He appeared pale and unsteady, and had not yet risen to his feet.

Yet he lived, curse it. She had not done her job well enough.

He leaned across the desk toward Catha and narrowed one eye. "Me, I always keep my promises," he rasped. "As you shall learn."

He turned his hot gaze on Tansy. She saw something amiss with his eyes, then—they no longer gazed both in quite the same direction and the white showed around the reddish brown, on the right.

"You attacked me. Stupid bitch. Moreover— moreover, you are a witch."

The man holding Tansy twitched violently.

Latham went on, "I do promise you will pay for both sins—in flesh and in pain. Take her to a cell."

"Nay!" Tansy erupted into a frenzy, panic fueling her remaining strength. Wildly, she fought the hands that held her. She kicked and flailed, and her captor grunted and grappled with her more strongly. A second man stepped forward to lend a hand which, in turn, caused Catha to leap into the fray.

"Subdue them," Latham roared.

The guards obeyed, using slaps and harder blows. Catha wept when they pulled her away.

"You shall no tak' her. She has done naught wrong."

"She has maimed me!" Latham pushed up from his seat using his arms; Tansy, half dazed, wondered if he were able to stand. "She employed black magic beneath my roof. She will be chained until I decide what best to do about it."

Chained.

Tansy's very soul rebelled. For someone who could endure only so much time confined beneath a roof, this prospect equaled pain. And there would be more pain to follow—great and unendurable pain. She thought of the cells where Malcolm and Mercien had been confined. She could not bear it. She could not—

She reached for her magic, but panic got in the way, and she could not grasp it. The guards pulled her away, and Catha reached out.

"Nay, listen! I beg you. I beg—"

"You will beg, Lady MacGunn," Latham returned harshly. "But it maun wait until after our wedding."

Tansy fought as she was dragged along the corridors, paraded past staring and fearful faces, but her strength swiftly waned. She heard the word *witch* whispered time and again, and many of the guards and servants gave the sign against the evil eye.

Tansy allowed all that to slide away from her. Only one thought possessed her mind: not the pit. The other cells, such as that where Mercien had been held, were places of horror. But the very idea of the underground cell stole her breath and loosened her bowels.

Not the pit. Please. I will do anything you want. Anything you ask. Please, God, if you exist...

They bore her past the kitchens, where more faces stared, down the stairs, and along the narrow passage where she and Catha had ventured before. Despite all her inward entreaties—or prayers—they stopped at the grate set between the stones.

"Open it up."

"Nay! Please do no' put me there. Please!"

"Would you rather be chained, stupid woman?"

"Aye."

"Toss her in."

Hard hands pushed Tansy, and she fell into darkness. The ground accepted her with a hard thump that brought a rush of pain. Ignoring the hurt, she scrambled up, parted her lips, and screamed.

****

"What is that?"

Better than half way to Crag Corvan, Malcolm drew up his mount to listen. Evening came swiftly, and he'd already begun looking for a place to stop over when the sound caught his attention.

"What?" Mercien returned without real interest. Malcolm could tell his brother struggled to keep his place on the back of the mount even though he strove also to disguise his weakness. Mercien was spent on a level at which, for all his own punishments, Malcolm could only try to imagine.

But he said, "A scream." His eyes widened, and his ears stretched. "There it is again—'tis a woman screaming."

"I hear nothing."

A chill stole over Malcolm's body, starting at his feet and spreading upward. Tansy. Could it be? But nay, far too much distance separated them.

From a physical call, aye. What if this traveled via enchantment?

He could not say what convinced him of it so completely, yet at that moment his heart became certain. He sat unmoving, staring between his horse's twitching ears while the dark came down, his heart telling him he needed to go back. That the woman he loved—*loved*—required him to return for her, weapons flashing.

What had befallen her? He did not know, but it must be dark, deep, and terrifying. Tansy Bellrose Gant did not break easily.

He could feel her breaking now.

At last Mercien stirred. "Brother, do you mean to sit here all night in the quiet?"

Quiet? But aye, her screams had faded. And by any road, how—how could he turn back? Getting Mercien home was and had always been his first responsibility. But by God, if Latham harmed a hair of that lass's head, did anything to cause her pain or dim the bright light in her eyes, Malcolm would see him settled, and personally.

"I believe she is in danger."

That perked Mercien up despite his exhaustion. "Catha?"

"Tansy for certain—perhaps both of them."

Mercien stared at him. He might well ask how Malcolm thought to know such a thing. Being Mercien, he said, "Then we maun ride back."

"Every part of me wants to. But for what purpose?"

"Rescue."

"How, brother? Without a troop o' men…"

"Yet 'twill take several days to reach home and journey back again."

"Aye," Malcolm agreed, his heart turning sick inside. "But as we both ken full well, sometimes sacrifices maun be made."

****

The stench of the pit—stomach-turning when Tansy was first cast in—seemed to fade even as her sense of smell became blunted to it. The reek did not smell fresh—instinct told her Mercien had not been held here. Instinct might still be operating; her mind was not. She screamed until she went hoarse, fell into the moldy straw, and wept inconsolably, not caring who heard. Despair held her in its fist, crushing.

Time passed inexorably, and exhaustion silenced her at last. Her thoughts stirred sluggishly at first, self-preservation lifting them like a ragged army. She took stock of herself.

Still wet from the loch waters and the rain outside, she shivered in deep shudders that shook her whole frame. Carved into the very rock beneath the keep, she doubted the pit had ever seen a warming fire—the chill of the place competed with the reek for supremacy. She lay, wept out, cheek on her hand, and wondered if she'd die from the cold. She hoped she might. It would make a kinder fate than any other she could foresee.

A chill might take her in her sleep. But she had strength and youth arrayed against that possibility, and an inner will she sensed she'd only begun to tap.

She wanted to die, aye, to avoid accusation and questioning. She wanted also to live, to see Malcolm again.

Malcolm. The very thought of him warmed her. She imagined she lay again in his arms, gazing into the dark heaven of his eyes. Joined with him as only a man and a woman could be, feeling the strength of him inside her, feeling too the balance they made together of light and dark, of mischief and steadiness. In Malcolm's arms, as never before, she became complete.

Now, torn away from him, she could only reach for what he meant to her.

Safety. Contentment so deep it had no words. Desire, need, and comfort.

Indeed, it seemed to her, while lying there in the straw with her life dangling by a string, all these things together made up love.

Aye, well, at least she'd had that a few precious times—had more than one enchanted night with him—before she died. She could carry that with her to the end, whether it came here in stunning cold or the other extreme of scorching fire.

She lifted her head from the straw and listened. The keep had gone quiet, save for the occasional thump of distant footsteps. The endless night—not in truth endless, no matter how she might wish—dragged on.

She wondered what befell Catha, whether Latham would seek to punish her. Then she pressed her eyes shut and summoned up the sole comfort remaining to her—an image of Malcolm's face, smiling.

Chapter Thirty-One

"It has been three days, my lord. I beg you release her and allow me to provide her with some care and warmth. Has anyone tended her? She may be dead, for all we know."

"She is no' dead. The guards ha' been listening and heard her weeping last night."

Tansy, hearing the two voices drift down the stone corridor and filter through the grate that admitted all she knew of air and light, scrambled up in a tangle of filthy skirts. She knew both voices. The first— Catha's—provided a thread of hope. The other filled her with icy dread.

Three days.

It did not feel so long, yet at the same time felt much longer. In all that time she'd seen no one—not so much as the face of a guard peering in at her. No food or water had been provided, and she felt weak and ill. After endless shivering, she'd begun to ache in every bone, and her throat burned.

Now she swayed on her feet, yearning upward.

"Catha!" she called.

"Tansy?"

She heard Catha start forward, and Latham's voice swiftly following.

"Nay, Mistress MacGunn, you will not. I ken fine how to break a woman—or a man, for all that. She will be better than halfway there. Do no' destroy all my work."

"Work?" Catha's voice, choked by what might be rage, no longer sounded recognizable. "Wha' ha' you done, besides leave her to die?"

"Do you ken naught about the art of questioning? I am but softening her before the examination begins."

"Examination?"

"She attacked and attempted to kill me. I ken full well what happened, but I will ha' her admit it before I provide justice."

"Admit?"

Latham raised his voice deliberately so Tansy could hear. "That she is a witch."

"Nonsense."

"It is no' nonsense, Mistress MacGunn. Everyone knows the country is infested wi' witches just now—and afire wi' the flames needed to eradicate them. Your wee companion, unwilling to submit, used witchcraft against me. I felt it. I need only cause her to admit her crime."

"How?" Catha sounded hoarse.

Latham gave a chilling laugh. "'Tis called persuasion. When she is ready, I will haul her out o' there and ask for her confession, given before witnesses."

"She will no' admit—"

"I assure you she will, eventually." Again he laughed. "As you will learn of me after we are wed, mistress, I can make anyone admit anything—even that which they may no' ha' done."

"I will no' wed wi' you unless you release Tansy," Catha declared.

Tansy's heart leaped with a sudden jolt of hope. But Latham's response dashed her instantly.

"You will, mistress, lest you wish to join her there in yon pit."

"I might wish it, over being wed wi' you."

Tansy heard the sound of a slap, and a gasp from Catha, quickly followed by her defiant words, "Aye— put me into the pit with my companion. I prefer her company to yours."

Another slap and a growl, "Keep a civil tongue in your head, woman, or you will learn the weight o' my anger."

"Do as you will. Until you release Tansy, I will no' agree to wed wi' you."

Catha must have broken free from him then, for she suddenly threw herself down at the side of the grate. Tansy saw her pale face through the rusted iron slats.

"Tansy? Are you there?"

"Catha!"

"Be brave. Be strong. I will see you released from there somehow."

She flew up and backward as Latham hauled at her. Tansy had one glimpse of his face before he drew Catha away. Only Catha's voice floated back to her, "I do so vow!"

****

"Father, we must speak together."

Malcolm entered the chamber where his sire stood at the window, gazing out. Chilly morning sunlight flooded the room, marking every line in Murgo Montgomery's craggy face and showing his age.

Malcolm knew full well his father had not slept.

Since Malcolm's arrival with Mercien yesterday, Murgo had rarely left Mercien's side, staying with him in the dispensary all last night. This made Malcolm's first opportunity to catch the man alone.

He had not slept either. He'd looked in on Mercien several times, always finding Murgo with his head bent over Mercien's cot. Between those visits he'd been haunted by thoughts of Tansy. By morning he knew what he had to do.

Murgo turned and looked at him blankly. His lips moved for a moment before the words sounded. "Brother Matthew says the eye was burnt from its socket, most likely wi' a hot iron. Tell me, son, why would any man—even Donald Latham—do such a thing?"

Malcolm had to gulp back the sickness that rose to the back of his throat before he could reply. "Hate," he said tersely. "Latham is all hate."

Murgo did not seem to hear him. "And to Mercien, of all men. Always laughing; always fair in his dealings wi' others. The sunshine in my life." Murgo glanced out the window again as if angry the sun should shine. Perhaps forgetting to whom he spoke, he grated on, "I love all my sons, but Mercien…"

Malcolm absorbed the blow, minor in the welter of pain he currently endured. He might be the elder, but he'd known forever his Da loved Mercien best. He could not blame him for that—Mercien held also a high place in his heart.

But perhaps with Tansy Bellrose Gant in the world, there might be one person who chose him first.

Did she remain in the world? That thought tormented and goaded him to speak on. "He will recover, Father. Mercien is strong."

"Wi'out one eye. Maimed and broken. My bonny son!"

"He is no' broken." So Malcolm hoped. Yet he sensed the change in his brother, bone deep.

Murgo rounded on him. "And the eye—the eye is no' the worst o' his injuries. I was there when Brother Matthew undressed him. That bastard laid the irons everywhere. Your brother may never father a son."

"I did no' ken." The sickness inside Malcolm rose in a wave. "He should ha' said. I would no' ha' let him ride so far."

"Your brother is made o' courage—pure courage. Of what are you made?" Challenge crackled in Murgo's voice like a whip. "Will you avenge him?"

"Aye. 'Tis what I came to say. I want to raise the household guard."

"You will need more men than that. Hire them if you ha' to. Empty my coffers if you must. Just bring me that bastard's head."

Generations of bloodthirsty Scot lay behind the words, and Malcolm responded to them. Yet a few shreds of sanity remained. "There is naught I want more. But you ken there will be retaliation. Latham is held in high esteem by the King."

"Bugger the King! Latham has harmed one of mine. I want him dead."

"Aye. And, Father, there is somewhat more. The lass I brought here to Crag Corvan, Tansy Bellrose Gant—"

"Eh?" Clearly Murgo, in his present state, did not recall her.

"She and Catha are still there, in Dun Ballan. I

need to rescue them."

"Catha, aye. She needed to be sacrificed for Mercien's sake."

Suddenly, blindingly, Malcolm wondered if his father would be willing also to sacrifice *him* for Mercien's sake. He did not ask; he didn't truly wish to know. "Yet," he said heavily, "I will see her free of that bastard's hands if I can. And when I bring Tansy back wi' me, I mean to wed wi' her."

"Wha'?" He'd snared Murgo's attention at last. "Wed? Who is this woman?"

A witch. A waif. A peasant from a village so poor it boasted not even a kirk. The heart of his heart.

"She comes of modest family but has great abilities in, among other things, healing."

"Wait a moment." Murgo's eyes narrowed. "Is she no' the one who turned my household on its head? I heard complaints o' her." He drew a breath and roared, "She is no one. You are my firstborn son. You will marry into a good family, worthy of continuing our line. 'Tis your responsibility—indeed, you should ha' tended to it before you went to France. What if neither of you had returned?"

Malcolm bared his teeth in a mirthless smile. "Then I expect the succession would ha' been left to our younger brother, or you would ha' needed to tak' yoursel' another wife."

"I am past that. And your brother may, as I say, ne'er have a son. It falls to you. If you will marry, we will decide on the right woman—as soon as Latham lies dead."

"Tansy—"

"Tansy? Take her awa' out o' that place if you

216

wish. Bed her if you must. But marriage? Do no' be daft."

"Father, I am no lad, but a proven knight. In this I make my own choice."

Murgo leaned toward him, his face stark in the merciless light. "Aye son, mak' your own choice. Just be certain 'tis the right one for the future o' this clan."

Chapter Thirty-Two

Tansy Bellrose Gant lay upon her back on the filthy floor of the pit, staring upward through unseeing eyes. A measured amount of light filtered down to her; it changed not with day or night, for neither reached this subterranean vault, but with the activity of the guards. When they came and went, they carried torches which shed radiance like mercy. When they spoke to one another she could hear their voices, though she could not always discern their words.

They had fed her yesterday—or had it been the day before? They'd thrown scraps of food down to her through the grate, but she'd touched none of them, most of which fell on a floor so rife with dirt she could not imagine putting anything that touched it into her mouth.

She no longer felt hungry anyway. But she wanted water with a thirst akin to madness. Later, they'd lowered a flask. The water inside tasted stale and musty, but she didn't care. She drank it all and wished for more.

Other than those dubious attentions, she might as well be forgotten. No one spoke to her or even glanced down through the grate when passing. Her condition steadily worsened. The shivering ceased, but the pain in her throat became a fire, and she burned with fever.

Mayhap, she thought now as she lay nearly too weak to move, staring upward, she would perish of illness here and never emerge from this place, save as a corpse.

And that might not be so bad—better, no doubt, than the fate to which Latham would subject her if he hauled her out.

She wondered why he'd left it so long. She would not expect a man such as him to postpone retribution. Softening her, so he'd told Catha. Or perhaps he wanted her to feel this helplessness, the creeping weakness, the certainty she would die in this hellish place.

She'd tried again and again to reach for her magic—to fashion a weapon from the only resource available to her—only to discover it no longer remained. Nay, but that was a lie: it remained with her yet, but it flickered, low as a flame nearly snuffed, and could not so much as stir the air of this place.

And she'd begun to suffer visions, things she knew could not be true. At first it had been mere snippets of dreams—or they might be memories, for she did not truly sleep. Glimpses of her father and Bessie—of Slurt in springtime, its bonniest season. She felt certain once, before she opened her eyes, that Malcolm shared her cell and bent over her, saying her name again and again.

Tansy, Tansy, Tansy.

Her heart broke when she opened her eyes and found herself alone.

But was she? Unquestionably; even the rats shied from this place—though, as her ravaged limbs could testify, the fleas abounded. Yet she became more and more convinced she shared the cell with someone. A shadowy form lingered in the corner, in the gloom where the light from the grate failed to reach. A dark personage, lurking. That, or an illusion.

But could one feel the company of an illusion? Perhaps what she sensed was the shade of someone who had died here—as many must. The scent of death fairly hung in the place.

From somewhere she found the strength to lift her head and stare into the corner. Its occupant stirred, and she caught a glimpse of a woman. Small and slender, she had long black hair, all tangled, and bore a number of wounds, none of them tended. Her face wore a grimace that bared small, white teeth, and her eyes shone silver in the gloom.

That is me. I am seeing myself. Only the woman looked older than she; faint lines marked her face, and an indefinable foreignness set her apart.

I am seeing myself in the future. Mayhap that means I will survive.

Difficult to imagine it at this moment. She tried to speak, to croak out a question to the woman, but words failed to form in her aching throat.

Am I going to die?

And a whisper floated into her mind. *Nay, Daughter, not quite yet.*

****

"Tansy! Tansy, are you there?"

Catha's voice issued from above and summoned Tansy from a very deep dream. She'd been with her mother, a woman she did not even recall, the two of them in this cell together. Or perhaps it had been a cell similar to this. Tansy only knew she'd tasted fear, bright and immediate as flame.

But she awoke from one dream into another, because she thought she saw Catha peering down at her through the grate. With all the light above and behind her, Tansy had trouble seeing her features, but her golden hair made a bright halo by which Tansy identified her.

"Are you there?" Catha repeated. Fear rode her voice, and Tansy realized Catha could see nothing but darkness in the pit.

Against the pain in her throat she replied, "Aye."

Catha exhaled a gust of air. "Jesu! Listen to me. I ha' no' much time. I bribed a guard to let me speak wi' you."

"Then speak!"

"Latham wishes to put you to death as a witch. He wants to do it here in the forecourt of the keep."

The terror that had dwelt inside Tansy for days uncounted reared up, lending her the strength to scramble to her feet. "And will he?"

"I do no' ken. I believe I persuaded him—" Catha's voice broke.

"To release me?"

"Nay—but to what I hope will be a better course, better for you, that is. I ken how cruel he is. You saw what he did to Mercien. You can but imagine what he will put you through before he allows you to die."

"Aye." Tansy swayed on her feet.

"He is no' yet recovered from your attack on him, and he is angry. But I begged and pleaded and reasoned wi' him and got him to agree…"

"To what?"

"Instead of putting you to death here, he will send you to the Royal Commission."

"What?"

"To the King's Commission at Aberdeen."

Tansy's legs promptly failed her. She fell into the

straw. "Nay."

"'Tis better, do you no' see?"

"Nay, I do no'! Nay, nay, nay!"

"Tansy, but list to me. Your trial there will be in the open, observed by many—not the horror Latham might provide you here. There will be certain protocols and men of reason. You may well be found innocent."

"Witches are no' found innocent. They are found guilty there and put to the death."

"You are no' a witch. Do you hear me? You are no'. You will tell them you are but a simple lass who has been falsely accused. Do you no' see, Tansy—there you ha' a chance. Here, you ha' none."

"Malcolm. Malcolm will come for me. He promised."

"He may well try. He would need an army to storm this place. At the Commission…"

"Malcolm can accomplish anything." His love for Tansy could. She found she believed that down to her soul. Love would save her.

"Aye, then mayhap he will follow after you to Aberdeen."

"What of our agreement? Latham needs to die."

"Whisht!"

"If he sends me off, you will be left here wi' him—you will be forced to wed wi' him."

After a moment's silence, Catha replied, "I ken. I am willing to accept that fate, in order to gi' you a chance."

But being sent to the Commission gave Tansy no chance—she would be back where she'd started. Aye, and mayhap her fate lay in the heated irons and leering faces of that forum. To die in agony and never see

Malcolm again.

"I am sorry," Catha whispered, sounding stricken. "I thought it best. Do no' hate me."

"I do no'." Would Catha's destiny be any less terrible than hers? Marriage to Latham, prey to his myriad cruelties lifelong. Perhaps the agony of the flames made a better—and certainly cleaner—choice.

Once the flames burned her up, she would feel no more, yearn no more, ache no more. But she would still love Sir Malcolm Montgomery, always and forever.

"I maun go," Catha gasped, and disappeared from the grate.

Perhaps I dreamed her. Just another troubling vision.

She spoke to the shadow in the corner. "Did you hear that? Was she truly there?"

No reply, which did not help Tansy reach a conclusion.

"Help me," she whispered to no one in particular. "Give me the strength I need to kill Latham before I die."

Chapter Thirty-Three

"Haul her up." The voice, harsh and merciless, issued from above. A number of shadows moved, obscuring the light, and Tansy heard the sound of metal scraping on metal. The grate opened, sending down a shower of dust motes. She backed up instinctively.

Someone thrust a torch down through the opening, and light flooded the space. Looking around hurriedly, Tansy saw that no one lingered in the corner—she was alone. She saw too the dirt on her hands and clothing; helpless dismay rose and nearly choked her.

The face and torso of a guard appeared, before a rope ladder came dangling down.

"Here, witch—climb."

Tansy hesitated. At that instant, her life seemed to hang in balance between the known—however terrible—and the possibly more terrifying unknown.

The guard snarled, "Come up on your own, or 'twill be the worse for you."

No doubt. They would take her out of the pit by force, perhaps beat her, carry her out with broken bones.

She grasped the ladder with shaking hands and began pulling herself up, so weak her feet fumbled on the ropes and her head swam. Before she reached the top, the guard seized her—one hand on her shoulder in a bruising grip, the other on her hair—and pulled her out the rest of the way.

Tansy screamed. Deposited on the stones of the corridor, she scrambled up and found herself facing Latham.

A man transformed. No longer able to stand completely upright, he crouched over a stick, gripped in both hands, and appeared to have aged dreadfully. Lines of pain bracketed his mouth, and a livid mark still showed in the center of his forehead—dark red—where Tansy had hit him with her magic. But the brown eyes looked the same—canny and cruel, full of hate.

Before she could speak, he detached one hand from the stick and, quick as thought, struck her. The blow took her in the side of the jaw, half spun her about, and nearly knocked her back down into the pit. Only the guard's hand, pinching her elbow, spared her the fall.

"Witch," Latham hissed. "You will pay for what you ha' done to me. Bring her."

Helpless, Tansy was plucked up and carried along the narrow corridor, up the stairs, and through the keep, with faces staring all along the way. They did not pass quickly, for Latham led them at a crab-hop, clearly struggling.

Amid her terror and pain, Tansy felt a thread of satisfaction over that fact. She had hurt him, and aye, she might well pay the price for it. But the bastard would never be the same.

And could she harm him one more time before she died? Had she the strength to accomplish so worthy a task?

Likely not.

Carried straight out of the keep, she squinted, nearly blinded by bright sunlight, the first she'd seen in days. The air, clear and cold, bit at her and swirled her hair like a ragged banner. She blinked dazed eyes and drew a sweet breath deep into her lungs.

The guard tossed her down on the stones in front of the door. In one direction she could see the yawning doorway of the keep, in the other the wooden bridge that led to the watchtower. Directly in front of her she saw Latham's feet, well within kicking distance of her.

She scrambled a prudent distance backward. She could feel the hate and ugliness pouring from him, and her senses, stunted by the pit, roused.

"Bind her in chains."

"Master?" Even the guard who had charge of her seemed taken aback. Tansy, visibly weak, must present no appearance of threat.

But Latham roared, "She is a witch, and dangerous. Will you defy me?"

"Nay, Master."

Seized and hauled up between two men, Tansy felt cold iron cross her breast and wrap around her arms, which were hauled behind her. She bared her teeth at the sensation, even as manacles fastened about her wrists.

"Now load her into the cart. Do it swiftly!"

Before the men could obey, an interruption came in the form of Catha, who ran from the open door of the keep, face white and feet stumbling.

Breathless, Catha cried, "I maun protest!"

Latham turned on her savagely. "But, my lady, 'twas your request, this. I but comply wi' your wishes. Did I not, I would burn her here, where I could hear her scream and watch her flesh sear."

If possible, Catha turned paler. She cast one look at

Tansy before turning her eyes away. "She needs tending first. Food and water. Look at her!"

Latham did so, turning his hard gaze on Tansy where she half crouched in the grip of the guards like a feral animal, nearly at his feet. For one breathless moment their gazes met—reddish brown and pale gray—in a glare of pure dominance.

And Tansy felt her power—missing for days—rise. Just as before, it seemed as if his hate called and summoned it, perhaps even fueled it, dry tinder to flame. Now she drew strength from the air around her, the sunlight, the stones beneath her, and even Catha's concern, which she felt flowing to her. Swiftly, swiftly, she shaped it into a ball of fire, one with her own scorching hate behind it.

Latham, believing her powerless, smiled. "Aye so," he grated. "She is filthy, broken. Bound for her death—the most painful of deaths. She will beg for it." To the men he began, "Take—"

He got no farther. The ball of hate and loathing struck him—not between the eyes this time, but straight above his heart. Tansy watched his face change, stretch and twist, crumble and collapse like something made of sand.

Many voices cried out as he stumbled, let go of his stick, and fell. Several members of the guard hurried forward to catch at him; for the moment, Tansy was forgotten.

Catha rushed to her side. "Quickly, come!"

But, spent, Tansy remained on her knees, unable to rise. The chains weighing her down felt too heavy, and weakness rushed to replace the expelled power.

"Dead? Is he dead?" More than one voice asked the

question. Had Tansy still believed in prayer, she might have whispered one.

But another replied, "Heart still beating, low and slow." The captain of the guard stepped in swiftly. "Tak' him inside to the dispenser."

"What of the witch?" asked one of the men who held Tansy.

"Tak' her on to Aberdeen. Those were the master's orders."

"Nay!" Catha took up a stance before Tansy. "I will no' let you."

The men lifted Tansy between them and pushed past Catha. When she whirled and came after them, another of the men laid hold of her, respectfully but firmly.

Tansy, deposited in the back of a rough cart already hitched to a horse, strained to look back at her. "Run, Catha," she bade. "Run and save yoursel'."

Chapter Thirty-Four

Latham's keep came into view through a swirl of mist, looking like a crouching black dragon puffing smoky breath. Malcolm, riding with a troop containing nearly two score household guard and other warriors— some hired—called a halt and narrowed his gaze on the place, testing the waters.

Noontime had already come and gone. The weather, following several days of strong autumn sunlight, had turned against them, with mist, rain, and now this damned fog.

Still, he was here and ready to face whatever he must—be it a battle at the gate or a full-out siege.

Yet...something did not feel right. The stone edifice before him appeared not only grim but lifeless. The portcullis hung half open; he could see no men stationed on the tower, no activity on the walls.

A frisson of unease chased up his spine, and he wished he had Mercien at his side. But Mercien lay back at Crag Corvan, struggling to recover. This fight, for Tansy Bellrose Gant, fell to Malcolm alone.

His immediate plan lay in issuing a challenge, demanding Tansy's release before setting fire to the tower and bridge. Then in the dead of night he and his men would swim across, slit whatever throats they must, and breach the walls.

Things would be much easier with the portcullis

raised. Could he be so fortunate?

Robert, head of his father's castle guard, rode up to his side. "Sir Malcolm, what do you make o' this?"

"Something does no' smell right."

"I maun agree. The place looks deserted."

"Aye. The tower guard were quick to challenge us last time. What do you think?"

Robert, a man in his late forties, had been with Murgo Montgomery a long while. He eyed the keep and agreed, "Somewhat is amiss here, aye. Could it be a trap?"

"They would need to know we were coming." Would Latham figure it? Would he expect a rescue? No question the man had a twisted and devious mind, but Malcolm could not see him laying such an elaborate snare on a chance.

Before he could decide, a call came from behind him and, at the rear of the troop, a furor broke out.

"Sir Malcolm, Sir Malcolm, a woman!"

Malcolm's heart leaped so violently it hurt. He spun his mount, peering back over the heads of his men, some of whom parted to let through a man, afoot, who supported a smaller figure. In the poor light, Malcolm could not see her clearly. She wore a shawl over her hair and limped piteously, leaning on his man's arm.

Tansy?

He drew a deep breath that contained a prayer. Let her be safe. Only let her be here with him, and he would never again ask anything. He would spend his life in making her happy. He would...

All thought broke off as the couple reached him, still with Robert at his side. The woman raised her head and put back her shawl.

He found himself gazing into Catha's blue eyes. Her face—white and strained—contorted and worked before she forced words between her lips.

"It is I, Malcolm. Only I! Tansy is gone."

****

Gone. The word continued to echo through Malcolm's head long after he rode away from Dun Ballan with Catha tucked on the saddle in front of him. It persisted while they chose a place to make camp for the night and lit a fire. Even after he instructed the guard and sat down with Catha, well-wrapped in a blanket, it continued to resound. *Gone, gone, gone.* As if his mind would not accept it, or as if the word itself foretold doom.

He glanced at Catha, who huddled, shivering, beside him, her hands clutching a mug of mulled ale. A woman transformed, she bore little resemblance to the poised and beautiful lass he knew. But the look in her eyes—haunted and shattered—overshadowed all.

"Tell me," he requested as soon as he felt her able to speak. The two of them sat out of earshot from the other men, and he'd waited patiently all this while since she'd stumbled out of the forest and flagged them down. His first priority must be getting her away, seeing her safe—he who had, in essence, delivered her into this nightmare.

Catha shuddered but, perhaps sensing the depth of his need, did not hesitate to speak.

"Tansy has been taken to the Royal Commission at Aberdeen. Latham sent her. I think…I think he may be dead, or dying."

Malcolm's lips moved, but no words came. The Commission. The very same fate from which he'd saved her when they met. He forced a single word. "When?"

"Two days? Three? I canna' tell, Malcolm. They took her awa' in a cart; she was in chains."

Chains. His wild, dark lass. Might as well chain a magpie and so break its heart.

A cart, though—a slow conveyance, and all the way to Aberdeen. Might he catch them?

"Think," he urged as gently as he could manage. "Was it two days or three? It might mak' all the difference."

"I…" Catha shook her head. "Three, I think. I fled, as Tansy bade me. I ran, and several of Latham's men pursued me. I hurt myself—fell. I hit my head and lay senseless for a time. I think that's also when I injured my leg. After that, I could no longer hear the men. I arose but managed no more than a few steps. I could no' guess my direction. When I heard your men ride through I crawled…because I heard your voice. Och, Malcolm!"

She began to weep, and he drew her into his arms, where she sobbed and struggled to speak words he could not catch.

Gone to the Commission. Days ago. Beyond his reach? He did not know, but dread filled his gut like a load of lead.

Catha swabbed her cheeks with the edge of her filthy shawl and struggled for control.

Only then did he ask, "What makes you think Latham may be dying, or dead?"

"Tansy attacked him, twice. The first time she hit him between the eyes, marked him, and hurt him quite badly, 'Tis why he put her into the pit—"

"The pit? No' the one alongside the cells where we were?" Horror nearly closed Malcolm's throat. The cell in which he'd languished had been bad enough. Many times he'd consoled himself with the thought that at least he was not in the pit.

"Aye. Och, 'twas so terrible! He would no' let me see her. The guards to whom I spoke admitted he'd afforded her precious little food or water. Latham's anger against her—well, I'd no' seen aught to match it. She had damaged him, see. Damaged him! He wanted to hurt her in return. He planned to kill her there at the keep—put her to the flame and watch her die. I pled for her life. For days and days I did, all while praying for a miracle."

Catha raised a shattered face to Malcolm's. "In the end, 'twas I persuaded Latham to send her to the Commission."

"You?"

"Aye, Jesu forgive me! I just wanted to get her out o' his hands. And I thought that there, at least, she would stand a just trial before sane and measured listeners."

"They are none of them reasoned or sane, Catha. You ken fine what goes on there." And Tansy, his wee Tansy, so full of life, in their hands...

"I do. Yet there is procedure. And law."

"The King's skewed law."

"Better than Latham's. You did no' see him, Malcolm. You did not observe to what level he'd descended. I argued for days, as I say—for nights—and at last convinced him the King would no' appreciate him taking power out of his hands. But then—"

"Then?"

"She attacked him once more. He ordered her hauled out of the pit, and ch-chained." Catha gulped and pushed on. "It happened right there in the forecourt. Latham's men had the cart all hitched, and they bore her out—she could no longer walk on her own. But she…she struck Latham wi' her magic again."

"Wait a moment. Struck him—wi' magic?"

"Aye. Did I no' say?"

"You said she hit him between the eyes—"

"With her power." Catha's gaze met Malcolm's in the dim light. In a whisper she said, "Tansy is, in truth, a witch. Did you no' ken?"

"I did." Malcolm nodded, feeling sick. "I love her full well despite it." Or perhaps in part because of it. When it came to Tansy Bellrose Gant, who could say?

Catha clasped his hand. "Then go after her. Speak for her if you can, be there when she is put to death, at the very least. Let her know someone stands for her— that she is no' alone." Catha shivered. "I think the only thing worse than the fate she faces would be the belief that there's no one to care."

"Aye, aye." But could he, who had faced a hundred horrors in battle as well as in Latham's accursed cell, face that? To see the woman he loved rendered helpless and to stand unable to save her. To watch her put to the death…

Yet he might be able to speak for her, as Catha said. And any chance, however slight, must prove better than none.

"I will send you back to Crag Corvan wi' Robert. Ha' you the strength to ride?"

"I will ride," Catha assured him harshly, "if you promise to chase after Tansy for me." She smiled grimly. "At least I ha' Mercien, at the end of my journey."

And what would Malcolm find at the end of his? The dread in his belly spread to his chest and made it hard to breathe.

"What of Latham?" he asked. "What was his condition?"

"I do no' ken, Malcolm. After Tansy's first attack—as I say, he did no' recover completely. It twisted and withered him—he could no longer stand fully upright and needed a stick to walk. I could tell he bore considerable pain. The second strike laid him out on the stones in front of the keep. I fled, no' waiting to tell if he lived or died."

"His men bore him into the keep?"

"They did. Others came after me. Do you think he lives yet?"

Malcolm shook his head slowly. "The place, Catha, does no' look right—no guards on the tower, the portcullis abandoned. Somewhat is very much amiss."

"Latham ruled with an iron hand. He maun be either dead or, as I say, dying." Catha's gaze touched Malcolm's again. "If he be dead, that is all the worse for our Tansy, is it no'?"

A thousand times worse. What, Malcolm asked himself, could save her from destruction?

Only him, perhaps—him and his love for her.

Chapter Thirty-Five

"Save me."

Tansy, her cheek pressed against still another filthy floor scattered with moldy straw, muttered the words one more time. After being hauled into this place—a fine stone building in the midst of a bustling town—she'd been brought before three men who eyed her like a bug and put her name on what they called a "schedule" for hearing. Since then, she'd languished in this cell, where she must have spoken the plea a thousand times. A spell it now seemed, an incantation. Something more than a prayer.

For all that, she could not imagine how she might be saved. Her mind had chased round and round, searching for possibilities, and found almost none. A lightning bolt might descend from the sky, rend the stones above her head, and allow her escape. A magical ladder might appear, letting her climb up through a likewise magically opened grate. A giant bird might fly in, peck open the grate, and seize her in its talons.

A simple, merciful death might come. It took her a day and a night to reach that conclusion. Her condition, as she assessed it, had become very poor. She'd been given little to eat or drink at Latham's keep and nothing since arriving in this second cell. She felt cold to the bones, wasted and weak, and the fire in her throat now made swallowing an agony. When she'd been tossed down into this pit, she'd twisted her knee and did not think she could stand on it. But she had youth on her side—or more rightly against her—and a certain vitality that bubbled at her heart. She did not think she was ready to die just yet.

She lay instead with thoughts teeming in her mind—hopes and fears, and what she supposed must be delusions. She'd been destined for this fate, from the moment she cursed Ranna Farquharson back at the market in Slurt. Or maybe since the time she'd been born. Who could tell? But fate had been inexorable, and even her love for Malcolm had not changed its course.

Malcolm. She thought often of him—her one comfort—and reminded herself at least she'd had him before she died. Nothing could take that from her, not the irons or the pincers or the cruel, staring eyes. She relived the pleasures they'd shared, over and over in her mind—how he'd touched her, joined with her, the wild beauty of it, and the look in his eyes.

No one in the whole of the world had ever looked at her that way. She needed to carry that memory with her, like the magical presence of her knight, to the end.

Yet it slipped away from her again and again, as fear took its place. Fear and delusion. When she'd been tossed down into this pit, it had contained a gaggle of women—old and young, fair and aged…they had been called one by one away to hearings, summoned by name and hauled up by the guards.

None had returned.

Quite apart from that was the presence in the corner.

Even in Tansy's debilitated condition, it felt familiar—akin to the dark presence in the pit back at

Latham's keep, with which she'd communicated. Moreover, she fancied that from time to time, when she allowed her eyes to close, she heard someone moving about, breathing.

Perhaps not the same, then.

She wished she had the strength to rise, and then felt grateful she hadn't. Mayhap she did not wish to turn her head and see.

Whatever the case, on this morning with the dirty light sifting in, only the two of them remained—Tansy and the other who might or might not be a woman. That meant one of them must be next to be hauled up out of here, destined to face judgment.

That thought made Tansy feel so ill she knew she would retch, if anything remained in her stomach to come up. When would the guards arrive? It did not matter if she remained unable to stand—some of the other women had been too weak to attain their feet. They'd been plucked out like baby birds from a nest.

How much would it hurt, what must follow? Would they coerce a confession? Could she hold on to a few shreds of dignity and keep from screaming at the end?

Save me.

Did she speak the words aloud, force them through her raw throat? She knew not, but something stirred within the pit, as if in response. Tansy heard footsteps, and a hand touched her on the back.

"Child, do no' weep."

Had she been weeping? She doubted it. But the woman's voice sounded soft, and very certain.

"There's no one can save you but your own sel'."

Tansy lifted her head, using every last shred of

strength, and craned her neck so she might look into the woman's face.

Wonder widened her eyes, so powerful it almost banished the weakness.

The face she saw was her own.

****

"Who are you?"

A ghost, a spirit, an illusion? Herself come back from some staggering, unrecognizable future to bring an answer, a warning?

The woman did not at once reply. Instead she laid hold of Tansy with small, strong hands—her hands, at least, felt real—and urged her into a sitting position. "Can you stand?" she asked then.

"I do no' ken. My knee will no' hold me."

"I will hold you. Come."

The place offered not so much as a stone bench— only the filthy straw and the bucket, now overflowing. But the woman led Tansy to the corner and helped her sit with her back to the wall.

Her voice, when she spoke again, sounded musical as the memory of song. "I stay here because when the guards look down through yon grate, they canna' see this corner easily."

"Oh." *And were you in the corner of that other pit, back at Dun Ballan?* Tansy ached to ask the question but did not quite dare. Despite their circumstances, this woman had an air about her that did not invite intrusion.

She asked instead, "Am I dreaming you?"

"'Twould be a braw thing, would it no'?" The woman waved a hand. "If we could dismiss all this as an ugly dream. But, child, 'tis not so. We are caught in the net like trout. And as I say, the trout maun free itsel'."

"How?"

The woman turned her face and gazed into Tansy's eyes, and Tansy lost all sense of the question just asked. The woman's face might, indeed, be her own, small and with sharp angles at cheekbone and jaw. Her hair hung loose, black as Tansy's but strung with silver threads. Small lines lay at the corners of her eyes and mouth. Her eyes…Tansy blinked and drew a painful breath. Silvery. Clear. As familiar as if she gazed into a mirror.

The woman whispered a single word. "Magic."

"I think I know you," Tansy said.

The woman's eyes crinkled as she smiled. "I believe I know you also. Only fancy! A gift, perhaps, now when we face death."

"So we do face death?"

"Quite likely, child. Most of the trout in the net do. Only the ones who can talk swiftly and cleverly have a chance o' making it back to the wide water. And we…" She let her voice die away before she concluded, "we ha' near run out o' magic, and all."

"Aye. I am ill. Spent. I can barely feel my magic anymore."

Something flashed in the woman's silver eyes. "Do you suppose they'd dare question such as we, did they no' make sure to steal our strength first?"

Tansy remembered striking Latham above the heart. "Nay."

"Nay. They ha' done this before, scores o' times, brought women such as we—and ordinary women also—to their knees before challenging them. All this is meant to reduce us, render us harmless."

"How do you know?"

"I ha' escaped capture some long time. Run up brae and down glen—lived wild, only to be snared at last, betrayed by one I trusted."

"One you trusted?"

"A man."

"Ah." Tansy thought about that, or tried to. It seemed her mind, cloaked in fog, could no longer see its way. "Did you love him?"

"Love. Now there's an interesting prospect. It can be strong or it can be weak. His proved weaker than I believed."

"I am sorry. 'Tis a terrible hard thing to trust someone wi' your heart, only to be disappointed."

"I ha' survived worse. I once survived leaving my own beautiful wee daughter behind."

Tansy caught her breath. "Who are you?" Though, aye, she already knew.

The woman ignored the question and mused on. "A bonny bit o' a bairn she was, if unco' fractious. She cried a great deal. Her father said she would settle; I thought no'. I kenned fine, by then, I would never settle, not truly. Something inside me bade me use my powers, and that in turn brought risk to him—and her. If I were accused, see, it would throw suspicion also on those I loved. I dared no longer stay wi' him. And that meant sacrificing her." The woman's eyes met Tansy's again before she said, "I hope you understand."

"What is your name?"

"Bellrose." The woman smiled once more, and silver light shimmered in her eyes.

Tansy's aching throat closed. A wave of emotion arose at her heart—wonder, longing, gladness, and grief—and her eyes filled with tears. "You are…"

"Do no' speak the word rashly; it carries too much power." Bellrose smoothed the tangled hair back from Tansy's brow with one small hand. "So—you are like me. I canna' tell you how many times I wondered. I wanted to come back and see, but I learned Drachan had remarried. Was she a good woman?"

"Aye, a very good woman." The longing became uppermost. "But you might ha' come back—for me."

"I might. But you ken, 'tis hard to tell sometimes what might be best for those we love. Sacrifices maun be made."

"Love." That word again.

"I always loved you. I am that glad I ha' this chance to tell you so, before the end."

Tansy wanted to believe her, this woman with the beautiful, silver eyes and the strong wisdom. She longed for it. But for too many years had doubt rested in her heart.

Instead she said, "Tell me about the magic."

"Ah, then." Bellrose took both Tansy's hands in hers and squeezed tight. "'Tis old—ancient. It has traveled down our line from mother to mother to daughter—crone to mother to maiden. Not every daughter is so blessed. I am glad to know you carry the gift."

"Blessed? How can you say so? It has landed us here."

"Child, many a woman has landed here who never dreamed of wreaking a spell. They have wept and suffered and died wi'out ever knowing the joy of being one wi' the world around them."

"What has the world to do wi' it?"

"Surely you ha' learned 'tis from the natural world our ability comes, and our strength. The air, the fire, the water, and stone."

"Stone is hard and unyielding," Tansy protested. "It keeps us in this terrible place. Water can drown. Air feeds the flame that will torment and consume us."

Bellrose laid her fingers against Tansy's cheek. "There are worse things than transformation."

"Eh?"

"The fire that consumes us will turn us into pure spirit. And then we will be everywhere—forever free. I want you to remember that, at the end."

"But, Ma…" Tansy choked over the word she'd never before spoken. "I want to live. To love. There is a man."

"Aye? A good one, I hope."

"Good to the heart. I do no' think he would ever hurt or betray me."

"Ah, Tansy, you are so young."

"You do know my name."

"Did I no' give it to you? And I ha' held it to my heart all your life long."

Tansy began to weep, the tears running down her face like rain.

"Come now." Bellrose put an arm around Tansy's shoulders and drew her close. "'Tis no way to meet your end, wi' weeping. Tell me you will go wi' your head high and courage in your eyes."

"I canna'."

"You can."

"I am sore afraid."

"Aye, so. Fear comes. So does strength. For such as us, strength means power. They canna' defeat you if you keep your head high."

Suddenly, Tansy felt her mother stiffen. Her face tipped up toward the grate. "Ah now—they come for one of us."

"Och no, no, no— I ha' just found you."

"Once found, never lost. Child—Tansy—look at me."

Tansy did, her eyes wide. She felt the connection between them blossom, silent but strong. "Daughter, I ha' given you little in life, it seems. Mayhap I can make up for that now."

Bellrose released her hold on Tansy, scrambled up from the straw, and stood on her two feet. She looked ready when the call came down through the grate.

"Mistress Bellrose."

The grate gave a groan as it was hauled open. Bellrose turned and gave Tansy one smile before the men hauled her up brutally, by the arms, forcing from her an involuntary grunt of pain. The grate slammed shut even as Tansy struggled to her feet.

"Nay—"

The word died away to nothing in her aching throat. She stood alone in the dirty beam of light that filtered down through the cruel, metal grate.

Chapter Thirty-Six

"I demand her release. She has done naught wrong, and stands innocent."

"Innocent?" The clerk who faced Malcolm over the polished wooden desk repeated the word as if he'd never heard it before, though he must have, a thousand times—in cries, shrieks, entreaties.

This place raised the hairs on the back of Malcolm's neck. From the moment he'd walked in, it seemed he could hear those cries and entreaties even though, in truth, he could not. Misery permeated the very air.

He glared at the clerk. The man wore a wig and a sour, supercilious expression. He looked both annoyed and confident in his position. Malcolm, not certain how to deal with such a dangerous authority, nevertheless knew one mistake on his part could harm Tansy's chances most terribly.

No diplomat, him. Used to battling with a sword in his hands, he usually only negotiated with men of the same mind. This exchange felt like a trap, and fraught with peril.

"Aye, sir, innocent," he repeated firmly. "She is my betrothed and has been accused falsely."

The clerk lifted his eyebrows. It had taken hours for Malcolm to achieve an audience with him; now it appeared he might be dismissed summarily. But the man pulled a thick sheaf of foolscap toward him. "Betrothed, eh? What was the name again?"

"Tansy Bellrose Gant."

The man began rifling through the sheets. Outside, a wagon pulled up, to the accompaniment of screaming. From where he stood, Malcolm could see through two doorways and just glimpse what happened there; burly men wrestled with an aged woman and dragged her from the bed of the wagon.

Not Tansy then. But nay, she'd already been hauled away into the bowels of this dreadful place. From one dungeon, at Dun Ballan, to another here.

He stood while the woman, her bloodshot eyes rolling like those of a panicked horse, was towed in between two men. They paused beside Malcolm, and he made full eye contact with the woman.

"Help me! I am no'—"

"Nellie Robertson," one of the men said to the clerk. "Witchcraft."

The clerk nodded and wrote the name and charge down carefully on the top sheet. The men hauled the screaming woman away.

Malcolm, turning cold inside, followed her with his gaze.

The clerk recalled him with a grunt. "Tansy Bellrose Gant, you say? Curious. I show two Bellroses. Not a common name."

"Two?"

"Your betrothed is charged with witchcraft. And murder."

"Murder!" Malcolm's thoughts flew. Latham must have died of his injuries. How to free Tansy now? "'Tis no' true, any of it."

The clerk leveled a hard stare on him. "If you would like to speak at her trial, you can wait."

"Aye. When?"

"I canna' say. The accused first must undergo questioning. A confession is always preferable, you understand. It saves time and also favorably impacts the accused's immortal soul."

Rage and terror suffused Malcolm in equal measures; the rage rose to his head and fed words to his mouth. "You think God listens? You suppose he can be found anywhere near this place?"

"Those who repent fare better in the afterlife: judgment above as well as below. Shall I make a note on the charge saying you wish to speak? Will you wait?"

"Aye." And how was he to discipline himself meanwhile? How wait without tearing the walls down? At any given moment, Tansy might be enduring the irons, making a false confession under the impetus of pain. Condemning herself.

She could expect no mercy. Neither, in the depths of his tormented soul, could he.

****

Time passed without measure while a host of thoughts crowded Tansy's mind. She thought about her mother and what might be happening to her, what agonies she endured. She lived again the wonder of gazing into the eyes of Bellrose Gant if, indeed, she still went by that surname, which Tansy doubted. She remembered how swiftly a connection had formed between them—or had it formed long ago? Mother to daughter, woman to woman, witch to witch. Whatever the case, she'd been able to feel Bellrose's spirit.

Curiously, she could yet, as if her mother lingered still in the corner of the cell. The energy felt the same as that which had occupied the shadows of the pit back at Latham's keep.

Was that possible? Did Tansy but imagine it all, a product of her terror and dread?

Would she be able to feel the moment her mother died? Transformed, Bellrose had called it. Turned to spirit. But the waiting dragged on.

She thought on the changeable nature of time—how a moment could fly in bliss or drag in agony. She wondered how it must stretch out when she lay beneath the irons—and then had to vomit into the overflowing slop bucket.

Try to vomit, that was. Nothing came up from her empty stomach, but the effort scalded her aching throat.

Perhaps I will die before ever they take me out of here. That might be for the best. But then she would never see Malcolm again—never gaze into his eyes nor touch his hand.

Ah—fool! That would never happen anyway. Best that the fever she felt raging through her body should take her. Best she should be carried out of here to her grave rather than to questioning.

Upon that thought, she heard voices and footsteps above, and a wailing cry drifted down the corridor toward her. The scuff of shoes preceded the now-familiar groan of the grate as it was drawn open.

A bundle of clothing tumbled down. Nay—it was a woman clad all in gray cloth and with a head of gray hair, like rags. She landed hard on the stone floor and her wailing abruptly ended. The grate slammed shut, and the guards marched away.

Company. But Tansy stood where she was, afraid to move or approach the new arrival, who lay so still.

Injured, no doubt—just as Tansy's knee had been injured when she fell that distance. None of their minders cared; there existed no one to help this poor creature. Save she.

Even as she acknowledged the fact, she thought she saw the woman move. Nay—something moved near her, a faint eddy that stirred the foul air. An exhalation? A mist?

Tansy approached her slowly and hunkered down as best she could, given her twisted knee. She touched the woman's shoulder. "Mistress? Are you sore harmed?"

Foolish question; to be sure, she must be.

At Tansy's touch, the woman flopped over onto her back. Her head sagged to one side at an impossible angle and her bloodshot eyes stared directly into Tansy's.

Sightless.

Tansy caught her breath. She'd seen enough chickens readied for the pot to recognize a broken neck when she saw one.

She withdrew her hand as if burned and got to her feet with difficulty. Forming the words through her burning throat, she called through the grate, "Here! She is dead! You canna' leave her. You canna' leave me wi' a dead woman!"

No response. Her voice did not so much as echo from the depths of the pit.

She backed off and retreated to the place her mother had once occupied, curled herself into a tight ball, and covered her head with her hands.

****

"Tansy Bellrose Gant."

The summons came out of near darkness and recalled Tansy from the place to which she'd retreated, one of fever and pain. It roused her and started her heart thumping in a mad rhythm. They had come for her.

At last.

She struggled to her feet and looked at the grate in dread. Here it ended—and here it began. She knew not what she went to face, nor all of what had happened to those who went before her. To her mother.

Only that it must be dire and terrible.

The dead woman still lay sprawled directly beneath the grate. The man who had come to fetch Tansy noticed her and muttered to another. One of them—after a cautious look at Tansy—dropped down into the pit, where he gathered her up precisely like the soiled clothing she mimicked. A rough ladder came down; the man handed his bundle up before gesturing roughly at Tansy.

"Go."

"I will no'."

Suddenly the pit seemed a haven of safety. Despite the malodorous air and its distance from freedom, she wanted to stay there. She reached for her magic—to knock this man down—and found only weak remnants that scattered from her reach.

Ah, had the spirit fled her? Did she go to this ordeal with no defense?

I abused my power. She knew bitter regret. *I wielded it against the likes of Ranna, and this is the outcome.*

Too high, too high a price. I never meant ill—well,

not much. Set me free and I will never again use the gift in order to harm.

"Move!" The guard shouted and dragged Tansy to the ladder, by the arm. He placed her on the first rung by force and gave her a shove.

She climbed. At the top, though, her legs failed her. She fell in a heap, a tangle of hair and filthy skirts, heart pounding so deafeningly she could not hear what the guards said.

Inexorable, they drew her to her feet and dragged her, by her arms, down the hallway.

Time, she understood, had all run out.

Chapter Thirty-Seven

"Stand there. Do no' interfere, or you will be turned from the chamber."

Malcolm nodded and pushed his way into the crowded hearing room. Night had fallen; torches flared around the perimeter of the place. Not so large a chamber as he'd anticipated, it must once have been a receiving hall, now well altered. Across the far end stretched an elevated platform hedged by a railing. There sat three men facing those who crowded in. The air reeked of too many bodies, and of fear.

Was this where Tansy would receive her hearing? Had she already endured questioning? By heaven, had she confessed?

If she had, Malcolm could not imagine anything he might do to win her free. A confession was a confession and represented certain doom.

Upon that thought, two guards brought in a woman, who shuffled between them. Malcolm's heart leaped painfully. Tansy? Only it was not she.

It looked like her—or as Tansy might appear some years hence. Her hair did, flowing loose and black about her diminutive face, awash with torchlight, and even the angle of her black eyebrows.

Not his Tansy, though. But whom?

This woman had clearly been through questioning. Now, unable to walk on her own, she dragged her way between the two guards. Deposited at the rail, she gripped it with both hands, in an effort to stand upright.

Malcolm pressed forward, earning glares and mutters from those around him. He ignored the dissenters. Something about this woman drew him—recognition? Nay, enchantment.

As he drew nearer he saw the marks on her—burns to both her cheeks, to her frail hands, to the skin revealed at her throat through gaps in her no doubt hastily assumed clothing. For an instant, across the distance, her eyes—clear and silver—met his.

Tansy's eyes.

It felt like a blow to the gut. He gasped and fell back a pace.

One of the men on the dais cleared his throat. "In the matter of Mistress Bellrose MacArdle, accused of witchcraft, we have obtained a confession."

Bellrose? Aye, and the clerk had said there was another. But how could it be?

The speaker glared at the woman at the rail, who returned his look stoically. She had just survived questioning harsh enough to elicit a confession. Malcolm, who had himself endured the irons at Latham's hands, knew what that meant. Yet he sensed strength in her, like a banked fire.

The speaker continued, "This Commission has been set up to do the King's work. It is also God's work. The eradication of evil lies close to our exalted King's heart, and he has instructed us to spare nothing in our pursuit of truth and justice. We are no' here to make false accusations. Many a confession heard in this place has led to the seizure and pursuit of other witches. This is as it is meant to be."

The speaker fell silent; the crowd muttered. The woman at the rail swayed and steadied herself. Her fingers turned white.

As casually as if he spoke of the price of ale, the justice continued. "This accused has confessed to both witchcraft and murder."

The crowd buzzed. The woman at the rail did not so much as blink.

"She is a powerful witch, and has admitted to influencing others. Under severe questioning, she revealed the existence of a pact with the devil, who supplies to her that power. She has given us a list of those she has harmed. She has accepted the consequences of her sins."

He leveled an eye on the woman at the rail. "Woman, do you confirm this?"

She nodded. Her eyes burned in her face like silver flame.

"Speak it out for the register."

"I do so confess."

Malcolm shuddered. Her voice, soft and roughened by pain, nevertheless struck a chord with him.

"You do, here before witnesses, confirm that as a powerful witch you ha' spread your influence far and wide? You ha' forced others to do your bidding?"

"Aye, so I have—others who are innocent."

"Bring in the other accused."

A door at the rear of the chamber opened; Tansy Bellrose Gant was brought in, also hedged between two men. All the breath fled Malcolm's body, and he pressed forward again.

She appeared unharmed. Weak surely, and filthy, her hair tangled and a flush in her cheek that drained away abruptly as she took in the setting. Her gaze swept the room, though she did not at first see Malcolm. It darted to the justices before fastening on the woman at the rail. Her lips parted and her legs failed her. She sank to the floor.

Inexorable, the guards hauled her up again and directed her also to the rail.

"Tansy Bellrose Gant," the justice intoned, "you are here to listen to your judgment."

****

Tansy grasped the rail in front of her with fingers that felt nothing. Neither could she feel her feet on the planks of the floor or her heart beating in her chest. She seemed to be outside her body, outside herself, aware of very little except staring faces.

And the woman next to her, near enough almost to touch.

Mother.

She'd been so sure she went for questioning, to fire and pain—being thrust instead into this place seemed incomprehensible. What had the man in the gray wig said? She was to hear her sentence. But she had not yet been tried.

Or heard. What could she say to sway anyone, with her sentence already decided?

After one swift glance, her mother had not looked at her. She stood unflinching and unmoving as a woman made of iron.

But Tansy could feel her: tangible weakness, a faint thread of power. Intent.

"Tansy Bellrose Gant, you have been accused of witchcraft and of murder. Do you understand those charges?"

"Murder? I ha' killed no one." Unless Latham lay dead. A curse on him if he did, and well deserved. She hoped he burned in eternal hellfire.

The justice pressed his lips together. "Do you know this woman beside you?"

"She is my mother."

Amid the throng of onlookers, someone stirred abruptly. Tansy looked toward the movement and saw Malcolm there, his face white among those of the other onlookers. Ah, impossible! Yet gratitude washed over her. She might well be going to die, but at least she'd had the gift of seeing him one last time.

"This woman, Bellrose MacArdle, has confessed to being a powerful witch. It is she and her kind whom the net spread by our worthy King is set to catch. She has stated she is able to"—he peered at the sheet of foolscap in front of him—"curdle milk, cause animals to be born with two heads, fly, curse her enemies with sickness, and bend others to her will. Her power enables her to act through the bodies of others, usurping their immortal souls, which she claims she has done to you without your knowledge. When charged with it under questioning, she confessed to the murder of a score of men including Master Donald Latham, of whose death you stand accused. What do you say?"

For an instant, all sense fled Tansy's mind. Beside her, Bellrose twitched violently; Tansy could feel her will. Comprehension descended on her like a shower of stones. Sacrifice. Her mother had spoken that word in the pit, had she not?

Now Bellrose's voice came whispering into Tansy's mind. *Daughter, let me do this for you. I am already lost.*

Beneath the impact of those words, Tansy crumpled and fell to the floor. Bellrose let go of the rail, stooped and raised her up again. They stood clasping one another—linked—and Tansy felt Bellrose's strength and determination.

Courage, child.

But you will die!

And you will live. I gave you the gift of life once before; take it from me again.

"Step away from her. Step away from the witch."

The room became loud with voices. Two of the guards started forward, and Bellrose stepped quite deliberately away from Tansy.

The justice bellowed for silence before continuing. "This woman, Bellrose MacArdle, does admit she used you and others, without their knowledge, to accomplish her foul deeds. She did confess this freely and clearly and on condition that you, Tansy Bellrose Gant, being innocent, should be released from this place and your accusation dismissed."

"No," Tansy whispered beneath her breath. "No—"

Hush, child.

The second of the justices scribbled firmly on the sheet that lay on the bench before him, and called out, "The prisoner, Tansy Bellrose Gant, is dismissed."

The guard at Tansy's right gestured roughly for her to leave the rail. Unable to move, she remained where she stood, everything within her protesting.

She felt a push from her mother, Bellrose's will shooing her away.

A stir in the crowd drew Tansy's attention to the tall man with the black hair, fast approaching through the crowd—Malcolm, his gaze fixed on her. He made his way to the rail and, after shooting one look at Bellrose, held out his hand. Tansy reached for it even as her heart broke in her breast.

As soon as their fingers met, she felt Malcolm's strength. It flooded through her, lifted her. A woman in a dream, she stepped down and allowed him to swing her off her feet and up into his arms, to bear her away.

But she craned her neck looking back—back—and met her mother's gaze. Silver on silver, woman on woman, heart to heart.

Remember I love you.

Which of them whispered the words? Tansy never knew.

Chapter Thirty-Eight

"She will go to the flame."

Tansy wept the words. She had not ceased weeping since Malcolm bore her from that terrible place and made off with her out of Aberdeen, just as fast as his horse could gallop. The back of his neck pricked all the way. After what he'd been through, both with Mercien and on his own, he'd lost faith in miracles. But he knew full well they'd just been delivered one, and he meant to make good use of it.

He still half—nay, more than half—expected guards to come riding after them, saying a mistake had been made and Tansy was, after all, doomed to the stake.

No question it would be her mother's fate. Her mother! Who would have thought they would meet in such a way? It almost seemed like magic.

But he worried for Tansy, who wept so inconsolably. She could not keep it up without harming herself.

Yet her lamenting continued to pour out. "She sacrificed herself for me."

"Aye." No denying it.

"I should ha' stayed and witnessed her end. I should ha' honored her in that way. She deserved that."

"Mayhap so. But Tansy, listen."

Malcolm slowed his mount, which blew hard. They

had reached open countryside well beyond the bounds of the town. No sight or sound of pursuit, yet.

He turned Tansy in the saddle, across his knees. "Your mother would no' ask that. She would no' want you to linger only to watch her die. She bargained for your freedom."

Tansy sobbed. "Aye, so she did. Malcolm, she must ha' endured the questioning—somehow—while keeping her wits about her. Made up that story about influencing me. Bargained to arrange for my freedom. How?"

"I do no' ken." Malcolm remembered the sizzle of hot iron against flesh, the screaming in the mind, the sapping of will. "She is a woman of prodigious strength."

Tansy peered past his shoulder down the rocky path. "We maun go back. Perhaps we can free her in turn."

"Nay, we canna'. Lass—lass!" He engaged her eyes, bright silver, swimming in tears. "Do no' throw away the gift she bought you at such a terrible high price."

Tansy collapsed in his arms. He felt the fever that burned in her skin, felt her extreme weakness and grief.

"I need to get you to safety. 'Tis the best way to repay your mother's sacrifice." He laid his palm on Tansy's forehead. "You are ill, burning up wi' fever. We maun get to Crag Corvan, where you can rest and grow well."

She held up her hands, piteous as a child. "I want to wash awa' the dirt—the feel of that place."

"Aye. Cuddle close, now. I ha' left my men at Dunbar. We will meet wi' them soon, and then we will be safe. Lass, can you hold on until we reach home?"

"Home." Her lips barely moved as she spoke the word. "Is there such a place for me?"

"Aye," he assured her. "Aye, Tansy—here in my heart."

****

"'Tis the fever will take her, if she goes." Catha let herself into the chamber where Malcolm and Mercien waited, and spoke in a hush. Since Malcolm, Tansy, and the troop of household guard returned home, the two men had spent the hours waiting in the study, speaking little.

Indeed, Malcolm had remained mostly silent all the while, though Mercien, on his feet and sporting a white bandage over his damaged face, offered all he could ask of sympathy.

Now Malcolm stumbled to his feet and stared at Catha. "You say I am to lose her?" Impossible, after all they'd suffered and endured.

"'Tis not I but Brother Matthew who warns of it. We ha' done for her what we can: cleaned the dirt o' that place from her and burned her clothing, tended her scrapes and bruises, and wrapped that swollen knee. Brother Matthew has given her draughts against the fever—she lies drenched wi' sweat—but it will no' break. She weakens, Malcolm. That is why he has sent me to fetch you."

Mercien made a sound of protest and moved to Malcolm's side. He placed a hand on Malcolm's shoulder and squeezed hard. "Courage, Brother."

Courage? Aye, and Mercien of all men had earned the right to speak the word. But Mercien had, still—or at last—his love. And Malcolm did not know if he possessed the bravery required to watch, should his own love die.

When had it happened, that he came to need her so? The first time he saw her, lashed to that post with all those angry faces hedging her round? The first time he touched her, kissed her? That first enchanted night they fused their bodies and spirits?

There must be some magic in it. She'd woven a spell over him, his wild, black-haired lass. Now he could not bear for that spell to break and did not think he could go on living if it did.

But nay, neither could he allow her to lie alone but for Brother Matthew, to die without him.

Catha, her eyes full of compassion, held out her hand, and Malcolm grasped it. They went together, all three of them, Catha still limping. Mercien—a bulwark of strength—brought up the rear.

The dispensary smelled strongly of herbs and powders. Brother Matthew, who'd at first been reluctant to admit Malcolm to the place, now stood aside for him. Not a good sign.

Tansy lay on a cot, all swathed in white, looking so unlike herself Malcolm had to blink. Her hair had been braided and tucked away under a close-fitting cap. Her face was damp and flushed red, and her throat ran with sweat. Her lips moved continuously, though her eyes remained closed.

"The fever will no' break," Brother Matthew told Malcolm, "whatever I do. We ha' given her every remedy I hold, and bathed her wi' cool water. Some evil lodges at her throat. I fear when it reaches her brain, she will pass awa'."

Malcolm, his gaze on the lass in the cot, did not so

much as glance at the dispenser. Matthew went on, "But she called for you. For you—and her mother. Can her mother be brought?"

"Nay." *Nay.*

"Then, Sir Malcolm, go to her. Let her know you are here."

Malcolm stumbled forward, no longer able to feel the floor beneath his feet. Destined to burn, this lass, he thought as he hunkered down and took her hand in both of his—either by flame or fever. It was not fair. They'd had so little time together, no more than a few nights.

He wanted her forever, for all his nights and days, wanted her making mischief in his life, shrugging off discipline and defying fate, being true to the irresistible spirit inside her.

"Tansy. Tansy, lass." He called her. His voice summoned her, as did his heart, yearning. His fingers on hers were an embrace, and a demand.

Her head, tossing on the bolster, stilled. Her face, all sharp angles without the softening billow of her hair around it, looked curiously foreign. So small and frail she was, to contain all his happiness.

"Tansy, love!" Did she hear him? How could he tell?

He tightened his fingers on hers. "Do no' slip awa' from me, lass. Do you hear? I command you to stay here wi' me."

Her eyelids fluttered. Her lips moved again, but he caught no word. What if she would not stay, if the magic between them did not prove strong enough? What could he say to hold her?

Mayhap he needed to weave an enchantment of his own.

A man of little faith, he. He seemed to have lost whatever he'd possessed in France, and in that cell of Latham's—and while looking into his brother's ruined face. But if he still believed in anything, it was in this scrap of a woman, the fierce ties between them, and the spell that joined them.

He whispered, "Tansy, lass, you maun hang on just until this fever breaks. 'Twill no' be long. Let me tell you what will happen after that—let me draw it all out for you in a braw picture. We will wed—aye, and I defy anyone to tell me nay. Any sort of joining you choose, wee lass—here in the chapel, in the grandest cathedral in the land, or out in a field—on a mountaintop—whatever speaks to your heart. And you shall be mistress o' my household—no one to tell you aye or nay. There will be children—och, such grand children! Wee strong laddies who will run wild wi' the ponies and learn to raise a sword and be true to the justice in their hearts. Bonny wee lasses so like their mother they will mak' a garden o' wee witches, spinning spells and spilling laughter through our days. And you and I—och, the love we will share, day after day! Night after night when I hold you and row you in my arms. We will grow old together, and never a moment's regret between us—you shall see it all, lass. All you need do is shed this fever and come awake."

Had he woven his spell well enough? Had he the strength? Had love the power needed to raise what magic lay within her?

Her lashes fluttered violently, and her fingers contracted on his. She heard.

She heard.

Chapter Thirty-Nine

Save me. Deliver me.

Did she lie in the pit, still? Nay, for they had dragged her out. She recalled most vividly the trip along the corridors and stone steps, her feet dragging, battered so severely when she reached the end of the journey she could barely stand.

The end of the journey. The crowded room, and howling voices. The cruel, avid faces.

Her mother's face. Silver eyes like her own, and a rush of warmth and strength.

Of magic.

And Malcolm had been there, by some bright miracle. More strength, and a sense of belonging so deep it claimed her very spirit.

But she'd left something vital behind. Her mother's magic. And her own?

Now she burned—not with flame but fever—and her throat ached fit to burst. She needed to search within, to find...that which she'd sought all her life long.

A voice, Malcolm's voice, poured into her ears, into her mind. *We will wed, aye.*

Wed—she and Malcolm.

There will be children, ah, such braw children.

Something within her stirred and quickened. A hint of magic arose at the core of her being, whispered to her just like Malcolm's voice.

And you and I—ah, the love we will share…

She drew a breath, fighting against the pain. Light exploded in her mind, and she could see it all—a trail of days and nights, laughter, warmth and enchantment. Permission to be the woman she truly was.

Suddenly she wanted it all—the beauty and the braw strength of it, the look in Malcolm's dark eyes. Her magic, a spring run nearly dry, welled up within her.

She felt a touch on her brow. Not Malcolm's—nay, not his. She opened her eyes and saw her mother kneeling at her side.

Gladness erupted inside her and, catching like a contagion, appeared also in Bellrose's eyes. "Mother. You are here—you did no' die."

"I canna' die, Daughter. Did I no' tell you I would be everywhere? In the air, fire, water, and stone—most of all in you, and those children you will bear your knight. But this—this is but a wisp of enchantment. A final spell for you." Bellrose smiled. "Call your magic to you. I ken fine you can. Even before you were, you were a witch. I bid you live your life for him—and for me."

"I am so glad I was able to meet you. I—"

If Bellrose had ever been there, she had now gone. Tansy found herself gazing instead into Malcolm's eyes; his hand and not her mother's lay on her brow. But the love—aye, the love was the same.

****

One year later

"'Tis a girl. Born lusty and hollering, with a shock of black hair to rival her mother's. I am a blessed man."

"So you are." Mercien clapped Malcolm on the back. "All is well wi' Tansy, then?"

Malcolm grinned. "Catha says she swore terrible oaths the whole time, enough to rend the air, muttered spells and, at the end, spoke to someone who was no' there." Though Malcolm had a fairly good idea who that might have been. "But she's fit as can be."

"Go to her," Mercien bade. He had barely a month to wait for the birth of his and Catha's first child—an event even more miraculous, given Mercien's injuries, than that which had just taken place. He burned with sympathy.

Malcolm did not need telling twice. He sprinted up the stairs to the chamber, where he found the midwife, who gave him a big smile, just clearing off. Catha passed him next, bestowing an embrace in passing, and in the room Malcolm beheld...

A scene of pure enchantment. Tansy, her hair wild and tangled, lay propped against the pillows in the bed, a tiny bundle at her breast. She looked bright-eyed and victorious, the very essence of woman.

Her silver gaze lifted to embrace him. "Come, see. Only look what you and I ha' done."

He sat on the edge of the bed and looked in wonder. The bundle had black hair, a red, wrinkled face, and tiny fisted hands.

"Another miracle," he breathed.

"Och, aye." Tansy passed her hand over the bairn's face; Malcolm thought he saw a glitter of light pass between. She looked at him again, a challenge. "You are no' disappointed she's not a lad?"

"I am no' disappointed," Malcolm replied, heartfelt.

"The next one will be a lad, I do so promise." Tansy lifted her chin. "The first needed to be a lass, you understand."

"Aye?"

"Och, aye—'tis a sacred trust. She and I will work hard, learn and spin magic together. This time, there will be no parting."

Malcolm, who rarely wept, felt tears gather in his eyes. "I've no need, have I, to ask her name?"

Two tears ran down Tansy's proud face. She shook her head. "None at all, my braw knight. I would ha' you meet your daughter, Bellrose."

Malcolm held out his finger; the bairn clasped it with her tiny hand. A tingle of magic traveled up his arm, and he smiled. "I do believe my life just got much more interesting. Welcome back, wee Bellrose." He bent his head to whisper, "And thank you."

A word about the author...

Multi-award-winning author Laura Strickland delights in time traveling to the past and searching out settings for her books, be they Historical Romance, Steampunk, or something in between. Her first Scottish Historical hero, *Devil Black*, battled his way onto the publishing scene in 2013, and the author never looked back. Nor has she tapped the limits of her imagination. Venturing beyond Historical and Contemporary Romance, she created a new world with her ground-breaking Buffalo Steampunk Adventure series set in her native city in Western New York.

Married and the parent of one grown daughter, Laura has also been privileged to mother a number of very special rescue dogs, and is intensely interested in animal welfare. These days while she's writing, you can always find her latest rescue, Lacy, nearby. Her love of dogs and her lifelong interest in Celtic history, magic, and music, are all reflected in her writing.

Laura's mantra is Lore, Legend, Love, and she wouldn't have it any other way.

Thank you for purchasing
this publication of The Wild Rose Press, Inc.

For questions or more information
contact us at
info@thewildrosepress.com.

The Wild Rose Press, Inc.
www.thewildrosepress.com

To visit with authors of
The Wild Rose Press, Inc.
join our yahoo loop at
http://groups.yahoo.com/group/thewildrosepress/